A Summer
of Horses

"Now, we'll try it again," said Beth. "This time you'll do it right."

"No," said Faith. "I *won't*. This is no fun. There's no reason why I have to learn to ride if I don't like it. And I don't." She thought of the three frightened faces watching them—felt she was speaking for them, too. Like an avenging angel, she cried, "This isn't school. I don't need a grade in horseback riding. It isn't *necessary!*"

"The Black Stallion is about the most famous
fictional horse of the century."
— *New York Times*

The Black Stallion
The Black Stallion and Flame
The Black Stallion and Satan
The Black Stallion and the Girl
The Black Stallion Legend
The Black Stallion Mystery
The Black Stallion Returns
The Black Stallion's Blood Bay Colt
The Black Stallion's Courage
Son of the Black Stallion
The Young Black Stallion

A Summer of Horses

Carol Fenner

•BULLSEYE BOOKS•
•RANDOM HOUSE•
•NEW YORK•

A BULLSEYE BOOK PUBLISHED BY RANDOM HOUSE, INC.

LIBRARY OF CONGRESS CATALOGING-IN-PUBLICATION DATA
Fenner, Carol.
A summer of horses / Carol Fenner.
p.   cm.—(Bullseye books)
Summary: Ten-year-old Faith struggles to overcome her fear of
horses and her feelings of jealousy toward her talented older sister
when they spend the summer on a horse farm.
ISBN 0-394-80480-5 (pbk.)   ISBN 0-394-90480-X (lib. bdg.)
[1. Horses—Fiction. 2. Sisters—Fiction. 3. Fear—Fiction.]
I. Title.   PZ7.F342Su   1989 [Fic]—dc19   88-31225

RL: 6.2

Manufactured in the United States of America
5 6 7 8 9 10

This book is for Esther
   singing to birds
And Faith with her honest
   eloquent eye
For beautiful Grace who always
   ran fastest
For Beth with her shoulder against
   the sky

Author's Note

I would like to thank my goddaughter, Jessica Rowe, who suffered through a tediously long draft of this novel when it was called *The Animal Person*. Thanks also to her mother, my good friend Susan, who helped her tackle it. Their reactions gave me fresh insight.

This book would still be called *Horse Story—Working Title*, but for my husband, Jay Williams, and my editor, Jenny Fanelli. On the same day and 750 miles apart they each came up with *A Summer of Horses* How could I protest such plottings of fate?

I am also indebted to my horse, Hail Raiser, who taught me how to listen.

Carol Fenner

*A Summer
of Horses*

No one was there to meet them. After scrambling to collect their luggage from the compartment under the bus, the two girls hauled their suitcases into the waiting room. There they stood in desolate silence watching the other passengers leave the station. The big room with its fluorescent lights seemed to grow colder and damper as it emptied.

"I think we should have gotten off at the last stop," said Gem, her voice dark with worry.

Faith glared at her older sister. "No way," she snorted. But she was worried too. They were supposed to be met by their mother's old college friend, and Faith couldn't remember what Beth Holbein looked like. The woman was a rare visitor to their home in the suburbs of Chicago.

She never talked much at their chatty dinner table.

"She might be late," Faith's mother had warned them. "She tends to pile too much into her day."

Their mother often talked about her quiet friend. Beth could lift enough bales of hay to load a truck. She drove tractors and a big horse trailer. If her old pickup truck broke down, she could lift up the hood and fix it. Faith's father said the reason Beth didn't get married was because . . . "Ye gods! She scares men away!" Beth could do many things that often only strong men do.

Perhaps this Saturday was one of the piled-up days, thought Faith. Or perhaps they *were* at the wrong station. Resentment that she had been holding in check rose up in her. She didn't want to be in this dismal, ugly station in the middle of rural Michigan. She wanted to be home, where her mother's fine voice hummed and sang through the tall rooms of their comfortable old house. She wanted to help her father do chores— empty wastebaskets and fold laundry, pick up twigs from their neatly tended lawn. She wanted to be home, where her brand-new twin baby brothers were just beginning to belong. They were tiny as puppies, with miniature fists and little curled toes.

I could have helped with the twins, she thought for the hundredth time. And Dad and I could have fixed the meals all summer. Gem would've been at the beach or on the phone. There's no way we would have been any extra trouble.

"Why isn't she here?" hissed Gem angrily and Faith snapped back to the present.

"Ye gods! What a place!" Gem's sour gaze swept the barren room and stopped at a door marked WOMEN. "I think I'll try the ladies' room," she announced and stalked off, her big canvas bag slung over her shoulder.

Faith watched her go with a mixture of envy and disdain. "Trying" the ladies' room meant her sister would comb her hair and brush her eyebrows and adjust her makeup. Gem was beautiful, with a lion's mane of sandy gold hair. Her real name was Grace Marie, after a great-grandmother, but nobody called her that. She was fourteen, a track star and a flirt. If there was no place to jog and no one to flirt with, Gem combed her hair.

Faith deserted the luggage to walk to the door and look out through the screen. It was late afternoon and the mid-June sun was soft in the parking lot. A gas station–store across the street had a dog-eared sign, OPEN, in the window. But no one seemed to be around. Down the empty street Faith could see a crossing where a dirt road met the paved one. Gem was right. What a place. Not even enough traffic to pave all the roads.

Gem came back more sour than before. "I hate this *farm* idea of theirs," she ranted. "I *hate* animals." She glared at Faith as if it were her fault instead of their parents'. "You should get along fine, you're such an animal lover. But *me*—I won't have any company except for a ten-year-old mouse brain."

"What about me?" cried Faith. "I've got a boy-crazy sister with bulging muscles and toilet paper wadded into her bra. Some company!" Then she added maliciously, "I think it's going to be great. You're such an athlete. You probably can do *chores* and stuff like that . . . clean out stalls full of *manure*. I think it'll be a perfect summer for you. Eleven weeks of horse manure!" The sisters glared at each other in the empty waiting room.

"You might just hunt up that number we're supposed to call in an emergency," Faith said, spite still nasty in her voice. "That is, if you haven't packed it in with your high heels and perfume!"

Gem slipped her hand into the depths of her canvas bag, rummaged around and haughtily produced a folded paper.

But there was no answer when they called the number from an old-fashioned pay phone. Faith had a dismal image of a faceless Beth waiting at another station in some distant town.

An hour passed. People began to arrive for the next bus. And Beth arrived, too. Faith recognized her from the window. She recalled the shining ponytail—hair the color of dark honey pulled back from the tanned face. But she also knew for certain it was Beth because she clopped into the parking lot in a horse-drawn buggy.

"She's here!" Faith yelled back to Gem, who had just begun to size up a tall, freckled guy wearing a basketball jacket.

Faith slammed out the door, her pale, thin legs flying, red hair floating out behind. The horse— a real, trotting, breathing horse! She'd loved horses ever since, as a little girl, she'd seen the mounted police parade in downtown Chicago.

"Hello," said Beth. "Thought you'd like a different sort of ride." She smiled a quiet smile and climbed down from the seat.

Faith's eyes were all for the horse, a chestnut—hair the color of her own. "Like new copper," her father always said. The horse's red coat had a burnished shine that deepened into shadows under smooth muscles. He stood quietly, but Faith sensed a readiness in his waiting. She sent him a silent greeting with her mind and eyes—as one animal to another. He tipped his head and slid her a sidelong glance.

Gem, who had finally torn herself away from the basketball jacket, came out the door with her snappy, self-conscious walk. Then she saw the horse and buggy. She stopped. Her mouth dropped open.

"Faith, Gem," said Beth, "meet Shinyface."

The chestnut's ears perked forward. People gathering to meet the bus stared with pleasant curiosity. This ordinarily would have embarrassed Faith. But Gem, the aggressive and daring sister, stood so dumbfounded that Faith was oddly comforted.

The buggy was old, but tidy. Its leather seats were worn. Beth grabbed the three biggest bags and hoisted them into the back seat. She was wearing old blue jeans, really old, not bleached out or faded on purpose but jeans with real holes in them, and big, thick boots. Faith noticed for the first time that, although Beth was slender with a narrow waist, she had hefty legs and strong, smooth arms.

Faith had never paid much attention to Beth when she had visited them. She had accepted her father's view when he claimed Beth was "crazy living all by herself—ye gods!—doing a man's job—never sure of where her next dollar's coming from."

Now, at this bright, exciting moment, Beth didn't seem at all crazy. She was the herald of lovely surprises.

The ride to the farm was splendid. Forgotten were the new baby brothers wiggling in their pretty blankets. Beth let Faith hold the reins. The power and pull of the big animal pulsed through Faith's thin arms as his great shifting hindquarters plunged them forward along the road. They drove beneath huge trees. An early summer breeze brought fresh meadowy smells across their faces.

"Fortunately, we've plenty of unpaved roads," Beth told the girls. "Dirt roads are much kinder to a horse's feet than pavement and a good deal less dangerous than our busy highway."

"You've got a highway somewhere?" asked Gem with an edge of sarcasm in her voice. She sat, surrounded by luggage, in the wide back seat.

Beth's answer was cheery. "Oh yes. Not too far. Civilization is within reach." Then she added seriously, "But far enough away to forget most of the time."

"Where do you go to the movies?" Gem asked in dismay. Faith wanted to add, "She means, where do you find the boys?" but she was feeling too good to bug her sister.

"We've got a movie house in town." Beth spoke over her shoulder. "It's open on Wednesday nights and Saturdays." Gem groaned.

"And I'm afraid my television is sort of sick." Beth didn't sound sorry. "But you'll never miss it."

The buggy rattled and sprang along. Gem slumped, sulking, in the back.

"Don't let the reins go slack," Beth told Faith. "Keep a light feel of his mouth."

Faith tried to sense the horse's mouth through the reins. Her special gift with animals had never included control over them. She had a fine ear for listening to animals—hearing speech in their voices. Part of her listening was noticing their movement, the expression on their faces, their eyes. She could creep up close to rabbits; she could scold back at a squirrel. Her father called her Dr. Dolittle.

They passed fields of new corn, a cattle ranch and more fields bordered by great oak trees. Faith kept trying to tune her listening in to the horse. But it was a bit overwhelming. Shinyface was so large and powerful. She contented herself with keeping her hands firm.

"How far do we go?" asked Faith. She felt an unfamiliar sense of command and she could have gone on forever. The summer spread before her, alive with promises.

"Almost there," Beth told her, holding out her hands for the reins. At a break in the line of trees, Beth slowed the chestnut and maneuvered the buggy onto a drive. Gem sat up, interested in spite of herself.

They approached a rattly, wooden bridge. Water sparkled and chortled beneath. Beth spoke soothing sounds to the chestnut, who drew his head down and arched his neck sideways at the busy water as they started across.

"Easy, Shiny, easy . . ." Beth murmured over and over. The buggy veered dangerously close to the bridge rail. Gem gasped. Faith knew an instant of panic. With high, tense steps, the horse pranced and twitched over the bridge. Now Faith had no trouble hearing the big chestnut. The signals were strong. She could almost see through Shiny's eyes—the water flashing and quivering like a great snake. A thrill of danger slid across Faith's skin.

Once on the other side, Shiny calmed down and trotted out quite smoothly. They passed a field with sheep in it. A big, old farmhouse came into view perched on a grassy rise. Faith noted it needed a coat of paint. Beyond the rise poked the top story of a barn, dark red with a sturdy roof. As they drew closer, Faith saw smaller buildings scattered about, all freshly painted. A stretch of grassy hills dotted with horses rolled up to the horizon.

Somewhere from these hills, Faith heard a wild, high-pitched whinny and the lower, calmer answer from a distant horse. She felt, beneath the sudden goose bumps on her skin, the stirrings of adventure.

$\mathcal{H}$olbein Farm was bigger than Faith had expected. Beth proudly informed the girls that the sheep they had just passed were hers and that the farm also supported many cats, three dogs and a donkey. Somewhere among the hilly fields were a small lake and several acres of woods. Her nearest neighbors, Beth told them, were a couple of miles away.

They drove past a corral where a gleaming dark horse trotted nervously. "That's Apollo, my stallion," said Beth. She explained that he was kept separate from the other horses "because he gets sort of crazy whenever a mare is in season."

"What's 'in season'?" asked Faith.

"When she's ready to conceive," said Beth.

"And sometimes more than one mare is ready at the same time. We isolate Apollo to protect him as well as the other horses—and ourselves."

Faith was just beginning to find the discussion fascinating when it ended. Beth's attention focused on easing Shiny into a turn toward the house. She halted the buggy by a sagging back porch. A huge, woolly white dog came joyfully padding to greet them. Gem stayed nervously in the buggy, but Faith slipped down from her seat and clucked and mock-growled. The dog's tail wagged furiously. She stroked his ears and scratched above his tail.

"Wolfie usually terrifies people with his friendliness," remarked Beth. She took a long, approving look at Faith before she turned to hoist the luggage from the buggy. Gem climbed down uneasily. She didn't care for dogs. She usually relied on Faith to keep one busy until she got away.

While Beth led Shinyface and the buggy down toward the barn, the girls lugged their suitcases into the kitchen. Wolfie panted eagerly at Faith's heels. "You stay here, Wolfie," said Faith, closing the screen door gently in his face.

Beth's house was a crazy jumble of things— "chaos" their father had called it. "You girls should get along fine in Beth's chaos, judging from the condition of your bedroom," he had said.

The kitchen floor was crowded with various kinds of boots—tall riding boots, muddy work boots, fat moon boots. Magazines, catalogs and unopened mail were piled on the kitchen table. A tangle of harnesses hung over the back of one chair. Dishes from past meals were balanced precariously in the sink.

Does our room look like this? thought Faith. She herself was rather inclined toward neatness. Her chair in their bedroom back home was piled as high as Gem's with soiled clothes, but hers were all folded. When she sat in the chair, it sort of pressed them neatly together. Gem created chaos around her, changing in and out of clothes and hairstyles until she only had time to drop her discarded things on the floor. "Dump and dash," their mother said of the older sister. "Miss Dump-and-Dash."

Now, at Beth's house, Miss Dump-and-Dash was looking for the bathroom, where she could lay out her makeup and colognes. Just off the kitchen was a large, modern, half-finished bathroom. Gem gasped and Faith followed her in. The bathroom was a mess. Back home there were rules about picking up towels and putting toothbrushes back where they belonged. I guess

Beth doesn't have any rules about the bath-room, thought Faith. Gem moaned.

The short laugh behind them made them turn around. Beth explained that one of her sheep had been sick during a spring frost and she had brought her in to keep her warm. The sheep had lain on the bathroom rug, messed on the floor, eaten from the bathtub and drunk out of the toi-let bowl.

"I cleaned up the worst part," said Beth. "I keep meaning to get to the rest, but I haven't found the time." The sisters just stood there speechless until Beth suggested, "Best to use the old bathroom just across the kitchen."

My, my . . . *two* kitchen bathrooms, thought Faith.

"Ye gods!" said Gem when she saw the other bathroom. A doorless linen closet was piled full of dirty laundry which spilled out into the room. A tall avocado plant sat in the tub, its leaves green and perky. Faith giggled. She wasn't fond of baths. Gem found the mirror to her liking and calmed down.

"You can explore the farm a little bit today, if you want," said Beth. "You'd better put on some boots." Then, noticing the confusion in both girls, she said that sneakers would do. "Did you bring any old ones?" she asked, eying their soft leather flats.

Faith and Gem changed into old tennis shoes right out of their bags, opened in the kitchen, and set out to explore the farm. Beth stayed behind to answer a ringing phone.

The girls, joined by the strangeness of a new place, stuck close together. They found a path down to the barn. It was a huge, old barn built into the slant of a hill. A short distance away was a fenced rectangle similar to Apollo's corral. There were no horses in it, just standing sections of fence and barrels on their sides. Faith grew excited. This must be the ring where riders practiced. They probably rode around those barrels—or jumped their horses over them! The ring looked as if it was used a lot.

They entered the barn into a room which Faith noted with surprise was clean and tidy. Saddles sat on wooden racks in neat rows. Bridles hung on the wall beside them. The room smelled of oil soap and leather. Passing through a narrow door between saddle racks, they discovered the stable. The odor of damp wood, manure and hay filtered warmly from a row of stalls. Faith peered into the nearest one and was disappointed to find it empty.

A ladder in the ceiling led into a giant hayloft overhead. The girls ventured up cautiously and climbed out on top through a square hole.

Hay was stacked in neat bales almost up to

the two-story ceiling. Light came dustily through little, high-up windows. Cats sat about, some of them stretching, some of them crouching, one of them clawing its way into a large bag of cat food. Faith thought this would be a cozy place to come with a book on a rainy day.

Next they wandered off to a field where they had seen some horses. "They must live out-doors in summer," Faith reasoned aloud. A number of them were grazing in the middle of the field. The girls climbed the fence and sat on top. The horses, after first looking up, bent their heads back to the grass.

"Let's go nearer," suggested Faith with a con-fidence gained from her ride in the buggy.

"Forget it," drawled Gem. "You're the big an-imal lover. Besides, Mom said to take it slow with big animals. And she meant *you*."

But Faith slid down from the fence into the field. Immediately she felt smaller; a faint chill of apprehension cooled the back of her neck. This was *their* field. But the horses continued to graze.

She stood for a while watching them in their field, trying to feel their life. Not one of them looked up.

Near her a butterfly flickered out of the grass. The sun shone down. Faith could feel the warmth rising from the earth beneath her. Insects hummed. She began to walk toward the group of horses.

Nearest to her was the big chestnut, Shiny-face, still wet from pulling the buggy. On his neck and hindquarters his hair was ruffled up and drying. He seemed enormous now that Faith was on the ground. Beyond was a small, pretty brown mare with a shaggy mane. A black horse bent his long neck quietly to the grass. The closer Faith got, the larger the horses loomed. She hadn't realized just how big they were. Tails switched at flies, horse skin shivered. The sun surrounded them all in a lazy peace.

Faith walked on a little slower, feeling her way. The black horse lifted his head and looked at her. She stopped and sent him her special signal, a little trembly with a strange nervousness. *Hello, horse.*

His gaze reached into her eyes, an alien stare. A quietness seemed to radiate from his body. His tail flicked. Faith could see, from the corner of her eye, the other horses raise their heads. They were all silent, looking at her, the intruder in their field. The sun beat down. The air seemed to grow thick.

Suddenly, without warning, the black horse spun up and around. His tail spread and his neck arched. His energy was like the crack of a whip among the others. There was a flurry and a springing and a lightning thrust of hooves. The horses bolted, twisted. Their necks tossed, manes flaring. A wild, shuddering cry came from the black horse. He stood up on his hind legs and pawed the air. His mane was like a flame behind him.

Then he plunged and bucked. His hind hooves struck out at the air. Faith froze in her tracks. Behind her, Gem screamed. Faith heard a thundering as the horses began to spin and wheel toward her. The earth seemed to heave beneath her. The pounding of hooves sent a beat up through her legs. Her body was rooted to the ground. Her scalp went cold.

The herd came boiling toward her. The air was full of the frenzy of their huge bodies. Faith heard a terrible wail rise up from her own throat, an awful sound she hadn't known she owned.

The sweat-wet chestnut was upon her. He wheeled and, flicking his hooves, passed by so close she could feel the warm wind he caused. Her arms flew up. As if at a command, the rest of the herd turned and raced in the other direction.

On weak legs, Faith ran lurching back to the safety of the fence. "Some animal lover," snorted Gem. Her face was so white that the few freckles on her nose stood out like crayon spots.

. . .

Later that evening, after a pizza supper, and after
the dishes were all piled on top of the dirty ones
in the sink, Beth said, "Tomorrow we'll have a
riding lesson." Gem and Faith exchanged looks
of horror. Faith felt an awful coldness coil in her
stomach.

Never before had she been frightened of an
animal. But these horses seemed so unlike the
groomed and bridled animals of the mounted
police. Even Shinyface in the field had not been
the same horse Faith had known harnessed to a
buggy. She could not understand what had
happened in Beth's field of unfettered horses.
Their great size and uncontrollable wildness had
filled her with terror.

"I don't think the horses like me," she said to
Beth. "There's a big, black one who didn't like
me at all." She described how savagely they had
behaved.

"Oh," Beth said, unconcerned, "they were just
feeling good, showing off for company. The black
one is Thundercloud. He was probably just welcoming you."

Faith was quiet, thinking about Thundercloud's welcome. His name alone was unset-
tling. He could have trampled her without even
noticing it. She knew danger when she saw it.

That night she dreamed she was in an empty

field full of the smell of horses. The air was heavy with danger. Suddenly the horses were there, pounding and thrusting toward her. She tried to make the right sounds—a whinny, a snort—but her throat was stopped. She turned and lifted one heavy foot after the other, pushing through the thick air with all her strength.

And woke up sweating and whimpering in the big bed with her sister. "Will you *stop* wiggling?" hissed Gem. "You're *ruining* my hair!"

Gem's irritation drove Faith's nightmare away. Comforted, she settled down in the bed and fell back to sleep.

3

*W*hen Faith woke up, the only trace of her fear was a vague uneasiness. The sun was sifting into the girls' room through pretty eyelet curtains. Except for two boxes of books in one corner, the bedroom was neat as a pin.

Almost as orderly as the tack room, thought Faith. She was warmed by the idea that Beth had made a special effort for them.

Gem was still sleeping soundly—her beauty sleep, their father called it. She tried to stay in one position all night so her hair would be manageable in the morning.

Faith thought she smelled French toast. She put on her slippers and followed the smell down the narrow, steep old stairs.

The grandfather clock by the door at the foot

of the stairs said 6:35, early for Faith. It's Sunday, she thought, and was struck with a wave of homesickness. Their father cooked breakfast on Sunday—pancakes poured into the shape of their initials. She wondered if her mother was awake yet. Were the twins sleeping?

Beth was at the stove when Faith wandered shyly into the kitchen. She looked as though she'd been up for hours. Her "Good morning, lazybones" was bright and crisp. A rich, nutmeg-y smell came from a grill next to the stove burners. It *was* French toast for breakfast. Faith's spirits lifted.

"Thought you'd be first up," Beth told her and then went to the foot of the stairs to holler up at Gem. "Wake up, Sleeping Beauty!" She sounded like their father. "You're getting old in bed!"

"I don't want to ride today," announced Faith while the three of them were eating breakfast. "Mom said to take it easy at first."

Beth pushed her French toast around the plate after the syrup. Gem tried to look cool.

"We won't do much," said Beth calmly. "Besides, Harold wouldn't hurt a fly . . . even a horsefly." She smiled at her own joke. "You'll see." There was something unbending as iron in her pleasant manner.

Beth got up and balanced her sticky plate in

the sink. "Put on your jeans and sneakers and I'll see you down below." Her voice was cheery but Faith sensed beneath it no room for argument. Without waiting for a reply, Beth left them at the table and headed for the barn.

Their suitcases were still in the kitchen, except for Gem's makeup case, which had displaced everything else on the counter of the old bathroom. They pulled out their jeans, clean socks and shirts and shoved their suitcases back underneath the kitchen table.

"I don't want to do this," muttered Faith as she dressed by the refrigerator. Her mother never insisted Faith do something against her nature and always seemed to know when not to push.

No matter how she lagged, Faith was finally clothed. Down below meant the stable in the lower part of the barn. The girls took their time getting there. Faith noted that the stable looked freshly swept. The smells that yesterday had filled Faith's nose comfortably, wood and manure and hay, now had a dangerous heat in them.

Beth was standing just inside the big stable doors with two saddled horses. One was the dainty brown mare with the shaggy mane and the other a big, strong-looking horse whose name, Beth said, was Harold.

"Harold is a bay. Bays are brown with black manes and tails and black legs." Faith noticed with alarm the great size of Harold's sturdy black legs, the huge, rock-solid hooves. "Harold used to be a hunt horse," Beth continued. "He really loved the chase."

"He's *big*," said Gem in her fussy voice which meant she was worried.

"He's old," said Beth. "And smart and beautiful." She leaned into Harold, her cheek against his shoulder.

Faith's body was growing formless with dread. Beth, who had seemed a new ally yesterday, was now a stone stranger.

"He's big," repeated Gem.

"But," said Beth, stepping away from Harold, suddenly all business, "Gem will ride Vixen. Faith will ride Harold."

Faith's stomach did a slow, horrible flopping. She would have to get on that monster. Beth handed her the big bay's reins and instructed Faith to follow her out to the ring. I was right, thought Faith, that *is* where riders practice. But no trace of her earlier excitement was there to comfort her. Harold was huge beside her, warm. She could feel him breathing.

"Don't let him step on you," called out Beth crisply. She walked out the door, followed by Gem leading Vixen. Faith leaned away from the big horse, reins loose in her trembling hand. She sidestepped out the barn door and banged her

shoulder painfully. Harold's feet seemed enormous, his body tanklike as he plodded beside
her.

In the ring, Gem was standing on a small
platform next to Vixen. A black riding cap sat
snugly over her heavy hair. ". . . left foot in the
stirrup. Swing your right leg over the saddle,"
Beth was saying. Her voice came to Faith as if
through a fog. "Hold the reins with your thumbs
on top." Gem looked as if she'd done it all before. Faith wondered where her sister's fear had
gone. She watched in surprise as Gem walked
Vixen on out around the ring.

"Pick a hat that fits," instructed Beth, point-
ing to a bin full of worn riding caps. "For your
protection." Faith was not reassured. Protection? With trembling hands she settled a hard,
velvet-covered shell over her head. It didn't feel
right—but *nothing* felt right.

"Lead Harold to the mounting block," Beth
urged a bewildered Faith. "To the right of the
steps—to the *right*." Then she added strongly,
"Always—*always* mount a horse from his left side.
Is that clear?"

"Why?" asked Faith, stalling for time. But Beth
didn't answer her question. She took Harold's
reins from Faith and led him to the right of the
mounting block. "Get on the block," she ordered. "Come on, don't waste time, Faith."

Faith, stung into action by Beth's sharp tone, mounted the steps. Harold didn't seem so big from this new height. It wasn't difficult to place her left foot in the stirrup and swing her other leg over the saddle. But once perched on the horse, she felt disconnected from herself, helpless. A warm, dusty odor rose from the powerful body. She could feel Harold's breathing, the readiness of his muscles. She herself had no muscles to speak of.

The big horse bent his head down and she felt as if she would pitch down his long neck to the ground. She clutched the front of the saddle. I'm not an athlete, she wanted to tell Beth, who was making quick adjustments in the stirrup leathers so they would fit Faith's ten-year-old legs. Everything was moving forward with Faith caught in the motion, her speech trapped in her throat.

Beth's firm voice came to her as if from a distance. "Now, just walk Harold around the ring after Gem." She clucked at Harold and gave him a quick slap on his rump. The muscles beneath Faith jerked and the huge animal walked.

Gem was proudly strutting about on Vixen. Sweat broke out on Faith's forehead and in the palms of her hands. The steady rolling heave of the horse made her feel sick to her stomach. All of her natural instincts, the parts of her that could exchange signals with animals, were smothered in a blanket of fear.

"You mount from the left because it's traditional," Beth's faraway voice continued. "The cavalry wore swords at their left side and couldn't swing that leg over the horse."

Ordinarily this information would have interested Faith, but she couldn't use it to eliminate the veil of fear she moved through. And Beth didn't seem to notice her fright. She just kept up a patter of facts about the cavalry and how they started the English style of riding and Faith no longer heard her at all.

• • •

The hour lesson was torture. Faith felt shapeless astride the huge horse. First Beth had them go clockwise around the ring. "Keep out to the rail!" Then they had to turn their horses and go the other way. Faith watched her sister learn how to post up and down as Vixen first walked, then trotted around the ring. Why standing up in the stirrups and sitting back down over and over enabled you to ride was a mystery Faith didn't even question. "Grip with your legs, Gem. Clamp those legs in and push up out of the saddle," Beth called out. "Up . . . down . . . up . . . down." Faith watched from the back of a slowly plodding Harold, hoping to be ignored. Now added to her fear was a rush of thick envy. I'll never catch up, she thought miserably.

Gem's face was serious with concentration. Up . . . down. Around the ring she posted, bobbing and bouncing unevenly to Vixen's quick trot.

"That's the idea," said Beth. "When you're posting correctly, the horse's trot won't bounce you all over the saddle. Feel that, Gem?"

Posting felt *impossible* to Faith when it was her turn. Even when she tried it at a walk, her legs chafed against the saddle. She couldn't rise up into the post without her upper body collapsing. Bored, Harold kept stopping.

"Keep him walking!" shouted Beth. "Cluck to him." The hair at the back of Faith's neck and around her forehead was wet from effort and anxiety.

Finally, with a sigh, Beth turned her attention back to Gem, whose athletic body responded easily to her directions. Faith sat rigidly on Harold and watched as her sister now posted evenly around the ring at a trot, her bright hair lifting and falling. Gem had the elated look she sometimes wore when running. Faith sat hoping Beth would soon call it a day. Walking Harold was awful enough. She didn't want him trotting.

But after Beth showed Gem how to halt Vixen, she turned to Faith. "Let's try posting at a trot,

Faith," she said with brisk cheeriness. "It's often easier than at a walk."

As if he understood the words, Harold moved into a trot. Fear swept over Faith. The quick, lurching movement shot her all over the saddle like a drunken puppet. The jouncing hurt her crotch. She hunched over the saddle, clutching the ridge in front of her. The reins dangled uselessly.

"Pick up the reins. Let go of the pommel!" called Beth. Faith barely heard. Whimpering, she bounced around the ring atop the huge animal. Her hands were glued to the front of the saddle. She couldn't obey Beth's shouted commands of "Look up! Look up!" Finally Beth told her, "Okay, Faith, let's walk for a while."

But now Harold didn't want to slow up and Faith couldn't make him obey.

"Pull back with the reins! Back with the reins!" Beth shouted. But Faith's brain was frozen. She could only clutch the pommel and whimper "Whoa . . . whoa" in a weak little voice. Her feet had been shaken from the stirrups. Her long, thin legs slapped against the horse's sides. Harold came to a halt in front of Beth.

Faith expected Beth to help her out of the saddle, but Beth just said matter-of-factly, "Why don't you walk him around a little? I'll work Gem and Vixen some more."

Harold plodded dutifully out along the rail. Faith watched her sister on Vixen. Gem had that greedy eagerness on her face that came over her when she was excited about something.

She's forgotten all about boys for an entire morning, Faith thought miserably.

At the lesson's end, Faith inched her way fearfully from the broad back, sliding down Harold's side, toes searching for the ground. Her legs ached. Her crotch was sore. But worse, she was shrunken with despair over her failure at riding. She led Harold back to the barn easily, though. Leading him was now less frightening than being on top of him.

"Cheer up," said Beth, seeing Faith's forlorn face. She unbuckled the girth and hauled the heavy old saddle from Harold's back. "Tomorrow you'll do better in a regular class."

Faith lay awake in bed that night next to her soundly sleeping sister. Gem had been too tired to do her nightly exercises or even chatter about "guys." Faith missed her mother, who would never have made her get on a horse. She felt somehow betrayed. She tried to think of a reason that would convince her parents, when they called, to let her come home. *I'm afraid of the horses.* She couldn't admit that. Here it was, only the next to last Sunday in June. She had two *months* plus two weeks to go before she would be back home where someone understood her. Gem's phrase, "some animal lover," burned like a brand in her mind. Faith staunchly resisted the urge to suck her thumb.

4

*T*he next morning Faith woke at half light. It was too early to get up but she couldn't get back to sleep. Aside from birds chirping sleepily, the farm was quiet. She lay there for what seemed like ages worrying about the day ahead. Then the sun began to slip through the curtains and she heard Beth running water in the kitchen. Monday the real world begins, she thought.

Without enthusiasm, she pulled on yesterday's jeans over the same underwear. She didn't bother to change her socks. Before going downstairs she poked Gem.

"Wake up, Sleeping Beauty," she said loudly at her sister's blinking face. "Time to clean out stalls."

She thumped down the stairs with Gem yelling after her, "You little rat!"

There was no French toast this morning. Beth was on her way out the kitchen door with a great bag of cat food in her arms and a cup full of coffee hooked by one thumb. She pointed with her elbow to the cereal boxes on a shelf. "Juice and milk in the refrigerator. Jam and butter, too."

She let the screen door slam, calling over her shoulder as she went, "Come down to the stable when you're finished."

Faith ate slowly, trying to hold the day still until she found her balance. She considered doing the dishes before she left the homey comfort of the kitchen. It would be a legitimate delay. She wasn't ready to be thrown on a horse again.

Gem bounced into the kitchen, jogged by the table and grabbed the piece of toast Faith had just loaded with strawberry jam. She banged out the door hollering, "Touché!"

Faith scrambled after her, forgetting the dirty dishes. She was furious at Gem. It made her feel suddenly brave and full of purpose.

But her purpose was deflated by the surprise of lively activity outside. Cars were pulling into the driveway, discharging kids of various ages in riding clothes or jeans and sneakers. Students for the regular classes, thought Faith. There were a few boys but mostly the students seemed to be girls. Faith remembered Beth saying that riding was one of the few sports where women could compete on the same level as men.

At the stable, Gem was finishing Faith's toast and sizing up a group of teenage girls in well-fitting breeches and long black riding boots.

"They're in the advanced class," she whispered as Faith came up. "We're only in the beginners."

Any of the remaining anger Faith felt toward her sister dissolved in a wave of panic. Before she could plan a quick disappearance, Beth handed her Harold's reins—attached to Harold.

"Beginners first," Beth said and added jokingly, "You can warm him up for the advanced riders." Faith, numb with worry, didn't even smile.

As she led the giant Harold down to the ring, her stomach churned. Mothers were sitting in their cars on the hill above the ring and more mothers were down leaning on the fence. Riders for the next class were chatting in groups. Someone's father stood with his foot on a rail, watching.

The warm face of Faith's own mother's face slipped into her mind. Tears began to collect behind her eyes. But Beth was now directing beginners to the mounting block, adjusting stirrups and clucking horses and riders out into the ring. There was no time for sorrowing.

Once Faith climbed onto Harold's broad back, her legs felt slack and useless. Added to the feeling of helplessness was embarrassment at being out there in front of all those parents. She felt naked and foolish on the giant horse plodding slowly around the ring.

Fortunately, there were seven other students besides Faith and Gem. Beth spent the entire first part of the lesson just getting some of them used to walking around while trying to post up and down. They all seem to catch on so quickly, thought Faith as she struggled in the saddle, following behind the only boy in the class.

"Posting smooths out the bumps when you're riding at a trot," Beth called out. "You don't tire as easily. You can cover long distances in comfort."

"Cover long distances?" Faith asked herself, imagining a prairie, a desert, endless hills. Around the ring was too long a distance for her.

But before the end of the lesson, four students, including the boy, were trotting and posting with Gem. Beth spent most of her attention on these riders. Faith and the other three were instructed to walk their horses around at the rail while standing up in the stirrups.

Faith's crumpled stance in the stirrups felt

unnatural and foolish. "If it doesn't get worse than this, I'll live," she said to herself. "But who wants to."

• • •

Toward the middle of that first week at Holbein Farm, Gem stopped describing to Faith the merits of all the boys she knew back home and began to talk about horses.

She doesn't even like animals, Faith thought dismally. Animals are *my* specialty.

Gem's conversation was now full of terms like "noseband," "throatlatch" and "diagonals."

Diagonals became one of Faith's nightmares. She could barely lift herself into a posting position at a walk. At a trot, she jiggled all over the saddle and her brain went cold. Now Beth was asking that she recognize diagonals.

"At a trot, horses' legs move in *diagonal pairs*," shouted Beth from the center of the ring. "Right foreleg with left back leg. And vice versa."

Faith's legs ached from the effort of trying to post.

"Notice when the horse's outside leg moves forward," instructed Beth. "Post *up* in rhythm with his outside leg."

The other riders seemed to be getting the idea. Of course the horse had only two forelegs—there was only a fifty percent chance of being wrong. But Faith *always* seemed to be on the wrong diagonal.

"Sit a bounce, Faith," cried Beth from the center of the ring. "Come up on the correct diagonal."

There was no time to think. It happened too fast. Faith couldn't distinguish one bounce from another. Desperately she tried to open her animal-listening ear, tried to feel Harold's legs. But she had lost connection with her *own* legs except for their twin throbbing.

"Slow down, Faith. Let him walk. You need to strengthen those legs," called Beth at one point.

With a sigh of relief, Faith pulled Harold down to a walk. That, at least, she could now do. She checked Beth's face as she and Harold walked past. Was she angry? Disappointed? The tanned face was quiet.

"Drop your stirrups and practice lifting yourself into posting position without them," said Beth reasonably. "Use the inside of your thighs and your knees. Twice around the ring. Cluck to him! Make him move out!"

Faith urged Harold into a faster walk. She strained and struggled to lift up without the stirrups to brace against.

"That's right, Faith, keep it up," said Beth. It didn't feel right but Faith felt she should get a Brownie point for fooling Beth. She couldn't raise up more than half an inch from the saddle. Still, she forced herself to keep at it. Twice around the ring seemed like forever. The insides of her knees felt raw.

When she dismounted to lead Harold back to the stall, her thighs shook uncontrollably and she felt close to tears.

Back in the ring she could hear Beth's crisp instructions as the riders went around one more time.

"That's it, Gem!" Faith heard. "Feel it?"

It seemed to Faith as though she were slipping into a dark and bottomless hole. Far up, at the edge of the hole, in sunlight, posted Gem on the right diagonal.

At suppertime, Faith was surprised at how Gem gobbled her pizza. She was usually finicky about food. She didn't want to gain weight. But that night Gem put away three pieces before Faith had finished her first.

"I think you're getting fatter," said Faith spitefully. "You'd better take it easy on the pizza."

"Mind your own business," snapped Gem, but her hand paused in mid-pounce over the fourth piece.

• • •

Thursday afternoon, Beth brought Vixen in from the field to show the sisters how to groom a horse properly.

"You girls can be a big help before lessons," she said, "if you know how to groom and tack up the school horses." Faith clenched her teeth and hung back.

"First, use the currycomb," said Beth. She rubbed deeply into Vixen's coat, circling against the hair growth with a tooth-edged rubber disk. Dust surged to the surface.

Faith found herself interested despite her nervousness. Beth showed them the various brushes, the different strokes to use to pull up dust and brush it away. Vixen stood quietly.

Beth had them each work on the mare.

"Don't be afraid to really brush hard," she said. "It stimulates the oil glands. Makes a shiny coat."

Faith hated getting that close to Vixen. But she couldn't brush hard standing stiffly away from the horse.

"She won't bite, Faith," said Beth a little impatiently. She took the brush from Faith and began to finish the job. "Vixen's been good," she said. "You can get her a carrot."

Relieved to get away, Faith hurried to the cool, shadowy part of the tack room where a big sack of carrots was kept. She had seen students giving carrot treats to horses before. She picked out a good-sized carrot and took her time getting back. Beth was knocking dirt and hair from the brushes. "You can give it to Vixen," she told Faith. "Careful of your fingers. Hold your hand flat."

Timidly Faith waved the carrot near Vixen's mouth. Vixen's teeth snapped open and caught it. Faith shrieked and snatched her hand away as the carrot disappeared, *crunch crunch*, gobbled by Vixen's nimble lips. *Crunch, crunch.* Gone.

Could've been my fingers, thought Faith, rubbing them. They felt dangerously like carrots. Can't even feed them right, she thought, sinking deeper into the hole.

She stood back when Beth showed them how to tack up Vixen. First Beth hoisted the saddle on and buckled it up. Then she picked up the bridle and slipped the reins over Vixen's neck.

In spite of herself, Faith edged closer. She was fascinated and horrified at the task of putting the bit into the horse's mouth. Beth stuck her thumb and fingers into the sides of the great rubbery lips. Vixen's mouth opened. Wet bits of grain and carrot slid out. Beth pushed the bit in between the big teeth and pulled the crownpiece in place over Vixen's ears.

It had taken only a few swift movements, but Faith didn't know how Beth made sense out of the noodle-tangle of leather straps she joined and buckled. Gem made a yuck-face when she tried putting her fingers into Vixen's mouth. Faith backed away, her brain closing off on the image of the big, wet horse teeth.

Beth sent her a long glance. Then, sighing, she suggested that Faith only be responsible for helping groom the horses and carry the tack. "You're not quite tall enough to pull the bridle over even Vixen's head," she said. Faith felt relieved and, at the same time, somehow cheated.

The next day, Gem bridled Vixen without a wince. Then, showing off, she bridled Harold for Faith. Faith was surprised and envious.

But in the days that followed, Faith did help with the grooming. Early every morning, before lessons, she worked hard, moving guardedly around the big animals with the currycomb, then the brushes.

Gradually she relaxed a little, no longer arching away from their warm bodies. Brushing became easier. She found herself enjoying the closeness and the healthy odor. Her animal-listening ear perked up. She began to murmur to the animals as she brushed. "Good fellow," she said to Harold. "Guh-uhd fellow." She forgot about being in a hole.

When she put away the brushes, her arms would be sprinkled with horse hair, her hands darkened by dirt. She always felt pretty accomplished until Gem handed her Harold's reins, saying with unctuous good will, "Have a good ride." Faith's spirits would sag. To get past the morning, to lunchtime and the easy afternoon, she would have to go through another lesson.

• • •

After lunch was the time that Faith enjoyed most. Things slowed down for her. Sometimes she visited the sheep, Wolfie panting at her heels.

Despite their blunt, stupid pushiness, Faith felt no fear of the sheep. She learned to call them, "Baaa-aaa," from way back in her throat. She began to notice their individual shapes and markings. When new-weaned lambs pressed to the fence, bleating for their mothers, she ached with sorrow.

At feeding time, she helped Beth carry pails of grain. She hoped Beth would notice how unafraid she was of the sheep. While Beth strode ahead of her, Faith chattered loudly about how she and the sheep were "pretty good friends."

Beth didn't wait when Faith had to stop and set the heavy pails on the ground to shake out her cramped fingers. Still, Faith thought she detected the stirring of a special bond between them. She longed to suggest that they hitch up

Shinyface to the buggy and let her hold the reins—as she had long, long, a hundred years ago. But whenever she had the words in her mind, Faith felt shy and told herself it wasn't the right time.

Some afternoons she helped Beth weed the vegetable garden. There were a lot of weeds but they came up easily from the dark, rich soil. "You're a better worker than your sister," commented Beth once. Faith turned her head to hide the surprise of tears in her eyes.

One day, Beth suggested Faith help Brady, too. He was a quiet, white-haired old man whom Beth hired to clean stalls, saddles and bridles.

Faith, pleased at being such a help to Beth, didn't mind the hard, dirty work. Since some horses were brought in at night, the stables needed daily cleaning. She swept out the aisles and tack room while Brady wordlessly shoveled out stalls and pushed wheelbarrows full of straw and manure outside.

Faith asked Beth what would happen to the manure pile. Would it just keep getting bigger and bigger? Beth was amused. "Oh, we use that to fertilize the alfalfa fields—and the garden."

Faith thought of the dark, rich soil around the thriving tomato plants, the growing corn and creeping squash vines. And the abundance of happy weeds. Everything went around in circles: alfalfa to the horse to the manure pile back to the alfalfa. Nothing ever really ended.

The lessons didn't end either. The second week, her sister was moved into a class with more advanced students Faith had to stay with children so small their feet couldn't reach the stirrups.

Beth now required that Faith bring Harold from the field herself. Fortunately, he was always standing by the gate waiting for the carrot Faith brought. She didn't have to step in among a cluster of horses to get him. The carrot Faith warily thrust at Harold served to occupy his attention while she snapped a lead line onto his halter.

Beth didn't approve of giving carrots *before* the lesson.

"That's bribery," she said. "Save carrots for a reward *after* the lesson."

But Faith always sneaked Harold the bribe. To her mind, she was rewarding him early.

Beth spent more time now urging Faith into a trot on Harold. Faith hated being with the babies who couldn't trot at all. She hated the wobble of her body in the saddle. But most of all, she hated the curling, sick feeling in her stomach that accompanied each lesson.

In the afternoons, she continued to escape to

the sheep or the other animals. She spent some rainy afternoons in the hayloft with the cats, a book and a peanut butter sandwich. She went for walks with Wolfie.

She talked with the orphaned baby raccoon who lived in the lambing shelter. His name was Rackity and, at first, he cowered in a corner of his cage whenever anyone came close. But Faith listened by his cage. She sat on an old milking stool and watched him for a long time. Soon she was able to coax him up to her hand. Rackity would let her stroke him. He got so he would take raw vegetables from her long, gentle fingers. Beth joked, "You must be part raccoon—a red-haired raccoon."

But Faith's pleasure in these other animals was somehow diminished. Her magic touch didn't extend to the huge, beautiful animals with their great, wet nostrils and heavy necks. Occasionally she wandered off by herself down to their field. She stared into it, leaning against the fence.

Beneath the peaceful appearance of distant horses grazing lay the powerful thunder of hooves, the uncontrollable strength of charging animals . . . lay violence and death. But here, too, Faith sensed, was some kind of an answer She had about eight weeks to discover it—or avoid it. She wasn't sure which she could do best.

5

In early evening, traffic on the dirt road past Holbein Farm virtually stopped. The quiet lengthened with the shadows. The sun eased down behind the woods. There was a comfortable munch from the feed troughs as most of the animals nudged noses to grain. It was the time Faith counted the days left of the summer.

Usually she sat on the back porch, scratching mosquito bites and listening to her sister splash in the tub inside. Gem's baths were as predictable each evening as the pizza. They were a kind of comfort to Faith. Wolfie always came and plopped down near her by the steps. That was also a comfort. Sometimes Beth came too, and sat quietly with them while the pizza baked. Then Faith felt as if she and Beth were connected somehow to the fields and hills, the animals, the softening sky. She forgot to count the remaining days.

Though Beth had finally gotten her television fixed, the girls had gotten out of the TV habit. The few times they did turn it on, the screen images were no longer compelling. The color seemed dimmer. "It's her set," said Gem. It's the horses, thought Faith. Beth herself never stayed awake in front of the TV very long.

Daytimes were a different story. Beth seemed to have endless energy. Activity was everywhere. Neighbors came to help build fences. Their voices and saws and poundings crisscrossed the air. Interesting strangers pulled up in cars to look over Beth's horses. People came with mares to breed with the beautiful, frenetic Apollo.

Faith observed the horse people with the detachment of an outsider. Serious young riders arrived with their fathers or mothers, wanting a well-bred horse to show at jumping events. Fox hunters from Midwest hunts and lean endurance-ride competitors came looking for horses with stamina. Sometimes they took a horse away, leaving Beth richer and sadder.

But Beth was too busy to be sad for long. She even taught classes on the Fourth of July. Faith and Gem didn't expect a celebration but Beth grilled hot dogs outdoors for supper. Afterward they lit sparklers and sat around watching them sizzle and die. Fireflies glowed here and there in the darkness. Faith wondered only briefly if her father had been fussing over his famous barbecued spareribs all afternoon.

Then Faith noticed Beth had fallen asleep, head on her arms, right where she sat. Beth's life doesn't pause for the Fourth of July, she thought. She was touched that this busy woman had made the extra effort to celebrate the holiday. Faith decided right then to find more ways to help at Holbein Farm.

• • •

There were plenty of things to choose from. Besides the grooming and helping Brady, Faith took over clearing dishes and cleaning up after each meal. She began to enjoy keeping the kitchen picked up. She organized the books and catalogs and magazines into several crates she had found in the unused chicken house. She kept Beth's mail piled neatly on her desk whether Beth opened it or not.

Gem caught the cleaning fever and began to organize the old bathroom, removing the avocado plant and dirty laundry. She arranged the towels by color and put the toothbrushes in pretty glasses. She wasn't feverish enough to actually *do* the laundry, but she sorted it and put it in baskets in the pantry.

"Now I won't be able to find things," said Beth, smiling.

"But you pick up the stables," protested Gem. "We can easily find bridles and lead lines because they're all put back in place."

Beth gave her thoughtful look again, faintly tinged with embarrassment. "Well," she said finally, "I'm only one person. Brady's only here a few hours a day. There is work here for at least three, maybe four. I have to choose the most important things as I see them. The horses can't clean up the stables or their bridles and saddles."

"You need a housekeeper," said Gem.

"You need a cook," said Faith, who was beginning to foresee the time when she would grow tired of pizza.

Beth sighed.

"You need a husband!" exclaimed Gem.

"Who can cook!" added Faith.

Beth began to laugh. "I see you two have it all figured out," she said, wiping her eyes.

"What kind of guy," Faith's father had snorted, "wants to move way out to a farm and be put to work by Beth, ye gods!"

Or made to ride Harold, thought Faith, silently agreeing with her father.

One day a young couple who had come looking for a carriage-driving horse hauled the high-stepping Shinyface away. They left behind a check for twelve thousand dollars. Gem was impressed. "No wonder Beth wouldn't let any of us ride him," she commented. Faith was sad when the couple drove off. They'd never hitch Shiny to the buggy now, she and Beth, and rattle along a dirt road. She watched the bright chestnut tail sway gracefully from the back of the couple's horse trailer as it disappeared down the drive.

Beth didn't see them leave. She had gone hastily into the house. When she came out later, her eyes were red and swollen. She didn't say a word to Faith but strode out to the field with a lead line and brought back Thundercloud. Faith watched her from the porch. The black horse followed, light and eager, behind the walking woman. There was something relentless about Beth's movements as she tacked up Cloud by the fence. She swung herself into the saddle from the ground.

Gem came out on the porch, waving fresh-painted fingernails. Together the sisters watched Beth ride through the field, up over the hill, and disappear. "What's wrong with Beth?" asked

Gem. "I thought I heard her crying in the sheep's bathroom."

"I don't know why she sold Shinyface if it makes her feels so bad," said Faith.

"She needs the money, dumb-o," grumbled her sister. "Dad says she always falls in love with her best horses and won't sell them and that she's broke all the time. Once she almost lost the farm because she wouldn't sell her favorite jumper to a famous rider for umpteen thousands of dollars."

"But she teaches," protested Faith, "and people pay her to board their horses here." And other things, thought Faith. Beth kept horses that were ready to foal and she helped in the birthing. Faith had never known anyone who worked so hard.

"She sells wool—and lamb meat, mutton and stuff," she reminded Gem.

Gem snorted. "Peanuts," she said. "Big money comes from selling her best horses. Dad says she has to shell out plenty for fencing and roofing and haying and farm equipment. And taxes. And vet bills."

Beth watched the spot on the hill where Beth had ridden from view. She saw the woman in her mind's eye . . . legs grown into the sides of the horse, a centaur, waist supple, hands easy.

Why didn't she sell that damn Cloud instead, she thought.

• • •

Strangely enough, Faith began to get used to Harold and his big bumble of a trot. The huge bay nuzzled her for a carrot and sniffed her hair while she snapped on the lead line. Other horses now recognized her as the carrot kid and edged closer for a treat too. Faith learned to throw pebbles at their legs to keep them away from the gate as she brought Harold through.

Although Faith still did not put on his bridle, Beth now insisted she saddle Harold after grooming him. At first it made Faith uncomfortable. She was afraid of angering the horse in her clumsy effort to heft the heavy old saddle onto his back. But Harold quietly tolerated her struggle.

She began to notice, brushing his round sides, that her listening ear seemed more alert. Not quite the way it was with dogs and the sheep. But she saw with new eyes Harold's smooth coat, his mane, the long muscles of his shoulder and thigh.

It was with surprise and a flash of fresh terror that she learned one morning that she would not ride Harold.

"He's sore in the foreleg," explained Beth. "You can ride Cloud."

Faith's heart stopped. Thundercloud! Her knees went weak. "Go get him," instructed Beth. "Go on . . . and *smile*," she added, seeing Faith's pale face.

Cloud wasn't standing near the gate. Holding a carrot stiffly in her fist, Faith walked slowly out into the field, a lead line over her shoulder. Her sensitive listening ear was filled with a low roaring. Cloud grazed off by himself, but Faith kept a nervous eye on the other horses, too. The big black animal looked at her curiously as she approached him.

"Cloud?" she said, her voice trembling. She stopped a distance away. "Hi. Remember me? I don't need any welcome today."

Cloud dropped his head and looked at Faith out of the side of his eye. She took a deep breath and walked slowly up to him. He didn't move. He eyed the carrot. She reached gingerly up to his halter and clipped on the lead line. He sniffed the carrot, then bit the end off daintily.

Surprisingly, the big black horse came in easily, almost eagerly. His eagerness itself was frightening. All her former discomfort around a horse returned as she was grooming him. His neck arched. His nostrils blew in and out. Warily she placed the saddle pad on his dark back, half expecting him to bolt. But he stood quietly as she hoisted the saddle on. After she had buckled it up, he stood staring out the door, ears alert.

When Beth came to put on the bridle, Faith was grateful. She still couldn't bring herself to put her fingers into a horse's mouth.

Once astride Cloud she immediately missed Harold's big, round sides. Cloud was leaner and there was a lightness about him—almost the opposite of Harold's solid steadiness.

"Hold on. Hold on a minute," Faith wanted to say. "Wait!" But part of her grew alive and excited. She didn't have to cluck to Cloud to get him to walk out along the rail. His walk was firm and easy. No lumbering here. His body coiled beneath her. And his trot, when Faith asked for it, was high and smooth as butter.

"I can still see a lot of daylight between your knees and the saddle," observed Beth loudly from the center of the ring. "Hug that leather! Knees in! Heels down! Grip with your *whole* leg."

During the lesson Faith found, to her delight, that she was posting easily up and down, working Cloud, at Beth's command, into a figure-eight pattern. She could almost *feel* the diagonal on Cloud and she tried to post up with his outside foreleg. Sometimes it worked. Faith smiled. She sat a bounce when they reached the center of the figure eight and sent him around the other way on a new diagonal.

"Good!" shouted Beth. "You've got it!"

Cloud was doing what Faith was trying to tell him. He felt wonderful. Visions of surpassing her older sister, trotting easily and with perfect control, filled her head. Her hands would be light, her legs would be strong. She ignored the flash of panic the vision stimulated.

"Heels *down!*" hollered Beth. "That's better. Now, give with those hands a little. Make them light. Pretend Cloud has eggshells in his mouth. Don't lose contact. Feel his mouth. And *relax*, Faith, relax. Loosen up that back. You're sitting stiff as a soldier . . ."

Beth hollered the entire lesson. She spent more of her attention on Faith than the four other students, little kids with astonished eyes. But when Faith was through it seemed like she had only been working ten minutes.

"That was much better," said Beth with a little smile. Faith slid down Cloud's side, enjoying for the first time the contact along the length of her body with the firm sides of the horse. The animal person in Faith blinked its eyes.

Later on, with no Beth around, Faith watched Thundercloud in his field. He flirted wildly with the other horses, plunging into their midst until they were all scattering and chasing each other, charging the air with an electric frenzy.

She was relieved when Beth put her back on Harold for the next lesson. Although she couldn't feel diagonals on the big bay, she was surprised at how much easier it was to ride him after Cloud—not smooth, but strong and steady.

There were only three other students in the class that day. They were all younger than Faith, and she felt pleased and confident to be way ahead of them.

"You're getting there," Beth told her. "You've come a long way. Time you learned to canter." She ordered the others to the center of the ring and told Faith to ready Harold. "You'll go counterclockwise," Beth said.

Nervously Faith listened to Beth describe the leg and rein signals that would make Harold surge into the strong, ground-covering pace. "Outside rein. Outside leg. That'll be your right. *Don't* yank the rein. Just a light pressure." But Faith's right leg couldn't work without her left leg. She couldn't give a strong signal with just one. Harold continued to plod around at a trot.

"I see daylight!" yelled Beth. "Hug that saddle . . . knees in! Knees in! Use your *whole* leg!"

Faith was mortified to be failing before the three younger students. They sat openmouthed astride their horses. There was so much to remember: knees in, outside rein, press with the outside leg. Which was outside?

Beth grew more irritated. She accused Faith of not wanting to canter and therefore not giving the signal in the right manner.

Finally Beth plucked a crop from the bin of hats. She cracked Harold across the rump with the little whip. He gave a huge lurch that almost unseated Faith, then shot around the ring at a canter. Fear flapped wildly in Faith's stomach. She leaned forward and clutched Harold's tough mane.

"Sit up! Sit BACK!" shouted Beth.

Harold's speed increased, his power exploding beneath Faith. All her control left her. Fear choked the scream back down her throat.

"Sit BACK! You're telling him to go faster! DON'T lean forward!"

But Faith no longer heard. Harold thundered toward the fence, swerved, and Faith slid halfway down his side.

"Sit UP. SIT UP! DON'T FALL! SIT UP!"

But down she went into the dust of the ring. Harold's great, plunging hooves narrowly missed her head.

She lay curled into a ball while the dust settled around her. Through a heavy numbness she heard Harold's hoofbeats as he headed toward the other end of the ring.

"Are you okay?" Beth was crouching beside her, looking at her intently. Then she seemed satisfied and said, "Just stay there a minute. Don't move. You didn't land very hard."

But I'm not okay, Faith wanted to say. I must have broken something, she thought. But at the same time, she knew she was not badly hurt.

Beth jogged over to Harold, who stood in the corner, snorting and blowing with excitement. She led him back to where her fallen student lay.

Faith uncurled slowly.

"Well, you've had your first fall. That puts you ahead of your sister."

My first fall? thought Faith. There's more to come? She stood up carefully. Her face was burning and her whole side felt stiff and aching. She was trembling and slightly disappointed that there was nothing worse wrong with her.

"We all fall," said Beth lightly.

"Even you?" asked Faith faintly. She didn't believe it.

"Yes," said Beth, "when I'm not being smart." Then she asked briskly, "Now, do you know why you fell?"

"He was going too fast," said Faith. "You hit him too hard." She became aware of the three younger students, faces pale and wide-eyed, at the other end of the ring. Harold stood obediently, but his body radiated eagerness.

"No," said Beth. "You fell because you *expected* to fall. You wanted to be on the ground instead of on the horse."

"I was just scared. He wouldn't stop," said Faith. She was beginning to feel belligerent.

"You were asking him to go," said Beth. She sounded exasperated. "You were telling him to go faster and faster."

"I was not," said Faith in astonishment. "I wanted him to stop."

"Now, we'll try it again," said Beth. "This time you'll do it right."

"No," said Faith. "I *won't*. This is no fun. There's no reason why I have to learn to ride if I don't like it. And I don't." She thought of the three frightened faces watching them—felt she was speaking for them, too. Like an avenging angel, she cried, "This isn't school. I don't need a grade in horseback riding. It isn't *necessary*!"

Faith's mother always left her daughter alone on the rare occasions when Faith balked or complained. Beth showed no such mercy. Her face was pale. Her mouth was straight.

"It is important that you get back on Harold *right this minute*," said Beth. There was nothing soft or gentle in her voice. But her hands were gentle. Her fingertips were soft on Faith's shoulders as she turned her to face the horse.

"Ready? One . . ." She bent and took hold of Faith's left leg. "Two . . ." And hoisted her . . . "Three!" up to the saddle. Faith had no choice but to swing her other leg over the horse. It was a comfortable, easy movement. Angrily she sat, staring through the big bay horse, through the dirt of the ring.

"Now walk him around the ring once," said Beth lightly. "Then give him the signal to trot."

Faith's face burned along the spot where the fall had bruised her cheek. Tears seeped from behind her eyes. Unwillingly she clicked Harold into a walk. She didn't want Beth to crack him with her crop again, so she pressed him into a trot. He was surprisingly eager, springing forward as though still inspired by Beth's earlier swat.

Sweat dampened the back of Faith's neck and grew wet tents under her arms.

"Twice around the ring," commanded Beth. "Don't let him walk. Keep him trotting." But after one turn, Harold stumbled back into a walk.

"I said TROT!" hollered Beth. "I want two full times around the ring at a trot. Start again."

Faith was furious. She hated Beth. But now, every time Harold showed signs of slowing down, Faith dug into him with her heels. Her knees felt raw. So did her throat from holding back her anger. Sweat was sliding down her spine and her shirt was sticking to it.

Faith finished trotting two times around the ring. She stopped in front of Beth and glared at her, daring her to make her do anything else.

Beth's face had a cold, closed look. She took a deep breath and sent it out sighing. "You can untack Harold and put him back in the field." Then she turned toward the other students, dismissing Faith, and said in a cheery voice, "Out on the rail, everybody. We're going to walk and then canter. Now, who can tell me why Faith fell off?"

As she left the ring, leading a quiet Harold, Faith strained her ears to hear what went on behind her. One student, a thin girl of about seven, piped up in a baby voice, "She didn't sit up."

"Little liar, nosesucker," said Faith fiercely to herself. She felt betrayed. It wasn't fair. The tears spread up again behind her eyes. "I will never get on a horse again," she vowed out loud, not caring who heard her, her voice slapping the air.

Harold seemed placid while she removed his tack. When she opened the gate to let him into the field, he hesitated, then nudged her shoulder gently, breathed into her hair. Faith burst into tears.

"Oh, Harold," she whispered as he moved off

toward the other horses, "oh, Harold, why did you dump me?" She hung over the gate, watching him amble away. "What's wrong with everything?" she mourned, half aloud.

Faith couldn't look Beth in the face that night. Beth didn't seem to be angry with her but the quiet easiness between the two of them wasn't there. Beth was coolly cheerful. She had made a delicious chicken pie for supper.

Afterward Faith and Gem helped carry grain to the horses and the sheep and paint one of the new jumps that would go into the ring. The anger inside Faith eased away, leaving a little rock of determination half buried inside her. "I will not ride."

6

*B*eth was getting ready to host a mid-July schooling show. The ring received a new coat of paint, fresh sawdust and bright pots of geraniums. Beth was preparing her students, too. They would be judged on how they trotted and cantered, how they started, halted, how they sat. They would be asked to ride a horse in patterns—a figure eight or a cloverleaf. Advanced students would take a course of jumps as well.

There was plenty to do without even getting on a horse. After her fall from Harold, Faith managed to disappear at lesson time for a few days. Her absence went unnoticed, or at least unquestioned, during the bustle. She pretended to be so busy stamping and banding the show announcements that time just slipped by her. But she knew she would have to confront Beth sooner or later, and she watched and waited for the smartest time.

Gem would ride in the schooling show. Eagerly she helped bring in horses for the lessons. She planned on riding in nearly every lesson Beth taught. She was "in training," she said. She wanted to do well against riders from other schools.

At night in bed, watching Gem do her nightly exercises, Faith listened to her endless chatter about the coming show. Gem worried about posting on the correct diagonal. Faith was surprised. She had thought Gem had diagonals down perfectly.

"The judge for the show rode with the Olympic team," Gem announced each night. In the same breath, she fretted that new boots, ordered two weeks earlier, had not yet arrived.

After her sister fell asleep, Faith would lie awake for a long time. She wished she were home. The phone calls from her parents were hurried and unsatisfying, with everybody trying to get in their say. Weekly letters came from her mother but they were addressed to both girls and talked about how the twins were growing. The funny lines her dad penned on the bottom made her feel lonely. She missed her mother's quiet "good mornings" and orderly breakfasts.

At home she could enjoy the squirrels and rabbits in their wide back lawn without being responsible for them. Here she was *forced* to spend time working around horses she didn't even like. Work, work, work. And Gem's whisperings at night, which used to bore her into sleep at home, now made her feel somehow crippled.

Two days before the show, she decided to approach Beth when she came upon her lying beside the lawn mower with the toolbox. A perfect time, Faith reasoned. Beth wouldn't want to spare any energy on Faith right now. There was mowing to be done.

"I'm not riding anymore," she said to the body bracing itself by the mower. Beth's face was contorted with concentration. Faith steeled herself and said stoutly, "I've decided I don't want to ride horses anymore."

"Just a minute . . ." grunted Beth. She gave her wrench one last turn and sat up, wiping her forehead with her sleeve. Then, to Faith's dismay, she turned her full attention on her.

"That's your decision," she said. "You're not an athlete like your sister. Your legs aren't strong. And you're not competitive."

That's settled, thought Faith, relieved and insulted at the same time.

"But," continued Beth, "you've a fine rapport with animals." She settled back thoughtfully on her elbows. "You recognize most of the sheep. Dogs follow you like children. You are easy with new mamma cats and you're the only one Rackity will come to." She looked intently into Faith's face. "Why not horses?"

"I can't listen to horses," said Faith. It pained her to say it out loud. "I know they're saying things, but I can't hear them."

"You've got it backward," said Beth firmly. "Horses are supposed to listen to you. You tell them what to do and make them do it."

"I can't talk to them either," said Faith.

"Part of talking to a horse is riding him," said Beth, standing up. "A horse listens to leg pressure—the shift of your body—your control of the bit in his mouth." She turned to go, the conversation ended.

Faith was silent, dissatisfied. Then Beth turned back to her.

"You ought to learn to lunge a horse, if you want to speak so they'll listen." Faith gasped as visions of forcing a horse to the ground, the way a cowboy twists a steer, leapt into her head. But Beth said, "You do it from the ground. With a long rope. It's a way of exercising a horse without getting on him." She turned back to the lawn mower. "Not now—after the show."

So, thought Faith, I'm not through with horses

after all. A knot of worry lodged itself inside her, but she pushed it away. Beth had said "after the show."

That night, Faith watched her sister run silently in place, knees chopping up high. "Does that really make your legs stronger?" she asked, sitting up in bed.

"I don't know," said Gem without missing a beat. She wasn't even breathing hard. "I just like to do it." She checked her stopwatch, though. Faith knew she believed in getting results from her efforts.

Faith got out of bed and tried a few jogs. Her feet slapped noisily into the floor. The bureau jiggled, shaking Gem's bottles and jars.

"Elephant!" hissed Gem. "Keep your weight up! Don't drop it. How can anyone as light as a bird sound like a mammoth?"

Faith *slap-slapped* a few more steps.

"Tiptoe it, mouse brain! Tiptoe it!"

"Tiptoe your big mouth!" cried Faith and flung herself back into bed. Gem began to do hamstring stretches, leaning her weight into her palms against the wall.

"That's why you're a good rider," said Faith. "Your legs are strong from running." She looked down at her own thin legs.

"Wrong," said her sister. "Different muscles

for riding. You keep your heels *down*, remember? Sergeant Beth's yell? *Heels down! Heels down!* You need to lengthen the back of your legs."

Faith watched. "This exercise is good for that," said Gem. "Or maybe walking upstairs with your knees in and letting your heels push down over the edge of the step . . ."

"Ye gods!" said Faith. "That sounds stupid."

But the next morning, while Gem was getting her beauty sleep, Faith tried running in place. She found to her surprise that, in trying not to wake her sister, she could "tiptoe it." She didn't last longer than forty seconds by her sister's stopwatch. She tried it again. She had never realized how long a whole minute was.

She decided, as she descended the stairway to breakfast, that she would run in place every morning before her sister woke up.

That night, she climbed the stairs with her knees together, her heels pushing down over the edge of the steps. It was awkward and she felt like an idiot. It took her forever to get to the bedroom, causing her sister to ask, "Where *were* you?"

"Nowhere," answered Faith, which was exactly where she felt she had been.

• • •

The Saturday of Beth's horse show they all rose earlier than usual, even Gem. Faith skipped her tiptoe jogging. They had horses to get ready. All week they had been mowing extra areas for parking vehicles from other stables. They had been laying down fresh straw in the stalls and cleaning tack.

Around 7:30 that morning, vans and horse trailers drawn by dusty big Buicks, jeeps and trucks began rolling into the farm. Faith had the job of guiding them to a proper parking spot according to a plan she had helped Beth work out the night before over a hasty pizza supper.

By midmorning she was high on her own importance. There was a circus bustle of people and horses about the place. Faith barely minded sidestepping the great, sleek bodies being led or exercised or groomed next to the various vans and rigs in the parking lot.

Guests from other stables, recognizing her as the red-headed parking attendant, asked her for directions. "Where's the water for horses?" "Where's the bathroom, miss?" "Where do I find Beth?" "Don't suppose you'd have an extra lead line."

She ran back and forth, finding a clothes brush for riders in their formal jackets, answering the telephone.

Gem looked elegant in a pale blue jacket with a dark velvet collar, but she pouted. Her hunt cap had a rip in it. Beth had assured her that the judge wouldn't notice it, but Gem had seen Beth's best rider in a brown jacket and matching velvet cap. Her name was Cora and she was a talkative show-off.

There was also a handsome boy from the LilJohn stables riding in the jumping class. He was tall and lean with very black hair. Gem tried to keep the ripped part of her hat away from his view of her. Faith told her, "He's not even *looking* at you." She wasn't quite telling the truth. The black-haired boy *was* checking her sister over. Boy crazy, thought Faith derisively. But she noticed that Gem was nervous and part of her sympathized with her sister.

Now Gem was fretting about making Vixen change leads when cantering the figure eight. "Vixen favors her right foreleg no matter which way we circle," moaned Gem. Faith knew, from hearing Beth holler it, that the inside foreleg was supposed to lead when the horse was cantering in a circle. The rider couldn't look down to check but had to *feel* whether it was right or not.

"I can never feel the lead," worried Gem. "I have to sneak a look down to see which shoulder is forward." She demonstrated, sliding her glance down without moving her head. "Could a judge notice my eyes?" she asked.

"I can hardly tell you're looking down and I'm standing right next to your face," Faith reassured her.

When Gem rode into the ring, Faith watched with Beth. "Wrong lead, wrong lead," muttered Beth when Gem turned in a figure-eight canter.

But her sister took a yellow third-place ribbon and carried it out of the ring with a triumphant smile. "If I can learn to feel the leads, I can take a blue ribbon next time," she boasted.

Part of Faith cheered her sister while another part mourned, "She's not even an animal person. She doesn't even *like* horses."

That evening, after the last dusty vehicle had pulled away and Beth's last tired horse had been turned out to pasture, Faith resumed the custom she'd forgotten the last few days. She counted the weeks until she could go home. But now there was a new, disquieting feeling. It won't be the same, she thought. Something is changing forever here this summer and nothing will ever be the same.

7

The morning following the schooling show, Faith's legs were stiff and sore from all the running around of the day before. But by lunchtime they felt supple and surprisingly strong. She went with Beth to bring in the horses for grooming and lessons. Together they climbed the long hill into the back field where the horses had wandered, grazing. Faith's fear at being deep in a field of horses was manageable with Beth along.

"I think I have more breath," she told Beth, bragging a little. "I don't have to stop to catch it."

"That's good," said Beth. "You can help me bring these fellows in more often."

Faith groaned inwardly. Why can't I keep my big mouth shut? she thought.

But as the days slipped toward August, Faith helped bring in the horses. Flies were thick about the stable. At the woods' edge, their forest brothers, deerflies, lurked ready to feed on warm horse bodies. The big animals stood in groups in the fields, whisking insects from each other's faces with their tails.

Each morning Beth broke through the clusters of horses to cull the ones she wanted for a lesson. She led three or four together back to the stables. Faith could only manage one at a time. She still sidestepped nervously when leading an eager Cloud or any of the other high-spirited horses.

In the back of Faith's mind flickered Beth's promise to teach her how to lunge a horse. Faith ignored it. Helping bring in the horses, grooming and saddling them was adventure enough. She also ignored the tiny spark of interest that glowed inside her like a small forgotten star. Lunge a horse?

Beth didn't forget. One cloudy afternoon, she asked Faith to meet her in the ring with Harold. He didn't need to be tacked up, just groomed, she said.

When Faith led the big bay down, she found Beth was standing in the center of the ring. Around her like the rim of a wheel trotted a frisky new dun horse, playfully shaking his head. Beth turned like a hub in the center, keeping taut the long line attached to his halter. With her left hand she trailed a lengthy whip in the dirt behind the trotting horse.

"This is a lunge line," Beth called to Faith. "The trainer's tool." She clucked to the horse and said, "Caan-ter." The dun horse moved from a trot into a slow canter. Beth kept the whip trailing behind him. The horse shook his head and sent out a playful buck. Calmly Beth brought him back down. "Tro-oh-t," she said. He slowed to a brisk trot.

Faith stood outside holding Harold by his lead line.

"You lunge a horse to exercise him," said Beth. Once more she clucked a canter at the dun, who tossed his head but began to canter again. He thundered in his wide circle about Beth while she turned herself slowly, following his movement.

"You lunge a horse to discipline him, too," said Beth. "You try and keep him balanced— keep his rhythm even." Faith watched the turning figure with a mixture of awe and worry. It looked easy enough. But then, so did riding.

"I want you to come in here," said Beth without taking her eyes from the horse moving about her. "Tie Harold to the hitching ring and come in here next to me."

Faith felt chills of panic cool her stomach. As she tied Harold up, her mind furiously planned how to dodge the circling horse to get to Beth. She sweated as she watched but, when the dun pounded past her for the third time, she dashed for the center.

"You lunge a horse to observe him," continued Beth as if nothing unusual had happened. "You also lunge a frisky horse to take some of the zip out."

Faith found herself turning beside Beth. With barely a change in movement, Beth handed the line to Faith. "Just keep it up," said Beth.

The transfer happened so smoothly that Faith had no time to panic. She kept turning while the dun cantered around her. He seemed not to notice the change. Beth trailed the whip.

"Now—gently—ease the line toward you," said Beth so quietly her words barely moved the air. "Don't pull or yank—just close your hand on the line, ease it in and say 'trot'—easy, now."

Faith closed her hand, her eyes fixed on the horse. His movement was hypnotic: *tha-thud, tha-thud*. She chose a moment.

"Trot," she said clearly, aiming the sound and easing the line toward her stomach.

The dun slowed down into a trot without a break in rhythm. A sweet wave of pleasure swept through Faith.

There was silence except for the soft thud of the trotting horse. They all turned together, the horse and Faith and Beth. Then Beth let out her breath.

"That was perfect," she said. "That was quite— perfect."

• • •

Harold was tougher to lunge, stubborn. It was hard to get him started. "Be patient," said Beth. "He knows the signals so well, he'll teach *you*."

But there was no repeat of Faith's success with the dun that day. The whip was difficult to drag while using the other hand.

"The whip just provides a frame. It's not to use on the horse—just to give him a boundary," Beth told her.

The entire process felt awkward to Faith. But gradually, in the days that followed, she learned to cluck Harold into a jerky trot around her. She also lunged Vixen and Cloud, a brown horse named Hobo and the dun. They were easy to work at a trot.

Cantering was another matter. The surge of power, the hooves pounding about her, touched the memory of wild horses plunging toward her in the field on that first day. She circled a thundering horse about her in a wash of dust and fear. Eventually, after many hours and many a horse, she learned to ease the big animals into a canter. But she had to steel herself each time she gave the *canter* command.

As her skill increased, Beth had Faith lunge high-strung horses before lessons. Sometimes Beth needed an older horse loosened up.

Once in a while, the lunging exchange between Faith and the horse became dreamlike. It only happened when no one else was about. The horse moved in a hypnotic circle around Faith and her commands came from her mouth like music.

"It's like we're dancing," she told Brady later. "And I lead." She had taken to talking to Brady, though he seldom answered her. But this time he said, "Wouldn't catch me messing with them birds. No sir, I don't tell 'em what to do an' they don't mess with me."

Brady's afraid too, she thought. She felt bold by comparison. Safely on the ground she could use her voice. She used her hands, too, caressing as she brushed the horses' smooth necks and sides.

She finally learned to put the bridle on the easy ones, working nervously beside the big, breathing bodies. Cloud took the bit with no fuss at all when her fingers pried into the sides of his slippery mouth. She remembered, in spite of herself, the feel of his eager response when she'd been astride his back.

"If you're really good, a horse sees out of your eyes—sees where you want him to go—while you use his legs to get there." Beth had said that, but it still didn't make sense.

What was it she had felt way back then on the eager black horse? Had Cloud seen through her eyes? Had his vision been clear and brave? *Could that have been her on Cloud?*

• • •

Except for five straight days of record-breaking heat toward the end of July, the Michigan weather was comfortable. There was a lot of rain, which made the grass and the trees lush and thickly green—and nurtured the flies.

Beth let Faith take care of the new litter of kittens in the barn, which included naming them. She hadn't suggested Faith take a lesson again.

Fine with me, thought Faith, but she did feel a twinge of jealousy and awe as her sister began to learn to jump a horse. Faith watched Gem on a small, gray horse first go over low cross poles and then over barrels.

She grew impatient with her sister too, when Gem fell in love with the feisty little gray, whose name was Rambler. All Gem talked about was

Rambler this and Rambler that. "He never pops a fence, that Rambler, he stands right off and goes over so smooth. And he's so *cu-u-te* and gentle, you'd never imagine he could jump that way."

Ye gods! thought Faith. But she could no longer say spitefully to herself that Gem didn't like horses. She just "lu-u-ved" Rambler.

Gem was also very excited over phone calls from the black-haired boy from LilJohn stables. His name was Owen. They talked for hours on the phone until Beth had to make a house rule about phone calls—twenty-minute limit or stall-cleaning penalties. This was very effective for, although Gem "lu-u-ved" Rambler, she didn't love mucking out his rich, odorous leavings from a stall. She began to set the kitchen timer when Owen called.

But if Gem had Rambler and a new boyfriend, Faith had seven kittens. At first they were kept in the pantry off the kitchen. The kittens were as good as twin babies, Faith thought, maybe better since they were tiny and furry and easy to cuddle. One in particular, the smallest and weakest, a black one with a white mask across its face, was her favorite.

The other kittens were strong and pushy. Blackie Whiteface, as Faith named the little one, couldn't fight its way to its mother's nipples through six other struggling bodies. Beth gave her a medicine dropper—"the nurse's tool," she said, and Faith used it to feed Blackie Whiteface watery milk with a little honey in it.

Beth gave Faith vitamins and other food supplements to mix into the milk. Soon the kitten began to fill out and grow, and Faith could tell that Blackie Whiteface was a boy.

Whenever Faith entered the pantry, Blackie Whiteface would come springing and wobbling in his dizzy little walk to climb all over her feet and claw at her socks. She would pick him up and he would crawl across her shoulders and back and grab at her hair. Once he wet on her shirtfront. Faith didn't really mind. Her animal ear was charmed by purring. And Beth seemed to be pleased.

Even after the mother and her kittens were moved into the barn, Blackie Whiteface continued to follow Faith. The first night he was away, Faith heard a mewling at the back door. There stood little Blackie Whiteface wanting to get in. He was so happy to see Faith that he clawed halfway up the screen door until Faith opened it and dragged him off.

Beth told her that, if she got Gem's okay, Blackie Whiteface could sleep in their bed. "Just one night," agreed Gem. But she was very agreeable these days.

The kitten wet in the corner of the room next morning and Faith hurried to clean it up. She spread some of her sister's cologne over the spot, hoping to discourage Blackie Whiteface from using the same place again.

Next night, Gem didn't say a word when Faith crawled into bed with Blackie Whiteface on her shoulder. "It's nice seeing you smile again," said her sister. "You've been so glum this summer."

Gem was having a wonderful summer. Excitement glowed in her face. She had never looked so pretty, and Faith felt only a little jealous. She had a cuddly kitten and she had noticed, as she did her hamstring walk up the stairs, that it was now quite effortless. Her legs were strengthening, she was sure of it. Perhaps she would surprise her parents when she got home. She wouldn't be able to ride a horse—but she'd have legs like a ballet dancer.

$\mathcal{E}$arly in August, Beth began to prepare her students for another horse show. Her patience was short during the lessons and she tolerated few mistakes.

"Now you *know* what a diagonal is! Why are you ignoring it?" Faith would hear her yell. Or to her prize student, Cora, who looked down at a fence while jumping it, "Where should your eyes be looking? Eyes up! Eyes up!" Sometimes Faith would hear her from as far away as the kitchen. "Relax. RELAX! Say that to yourself. OUT LOUD! I want to hear you say it." Faith could never hear the students from the kitchen, but she knew they were riding around the ring mumbling, "Relax . . . relax . . . relax . . .

relax." Washing up the breakfast dishes or watering the garden, Faith felt a little like Cinderella—doing all the unexciting chores while Beth's students were dressing for the ball.

"Easy with those reins; you're on his MOUTH! You're guiding a HORSE, not sawing down a tree!"

The lessons themselves, usually an hour, sometimes went on and on, lasting nearly two hours. The students were exhausted and downcast. Gem, whose smart new boots were rubbing sores at her ankles, was doubly miserable.

This horse show was a big one held at an elegant fox hunt stable near Detroit. Riders from many Midwest states, the East Coast and even Canada were coming. Beth would have to truck the horses a long distance and they would not return until after midnight. Beth said Gem was ready to compete in a jumping class as well as on the flat.

As the show date grew closer, Faith too was caught in the fever of preparations. She cleaned and oiled tack, washed saddle pads and helped the riding students with the daily grooming of the four horses that would be used in the show.

Faith admired clever, quick Cora, Beth's best rider. She was nervous and funny and talked as she groomed about riding disasters—falls she'd

had and bad habits of horses. Faith wondered
how she could keep riding in the face of so much
danger.

At night Faith went gradually to sleep amid
the restless, excited chatter of her sister. Gem
was trying to hypnotize herself into the correct
jumping position. "Hands forward, eyes forward—heels down." She repeated it over and
over to herself. As her voice droned away, sleep
came slowly and deliciously to Faith, snuggled
next to Blackie Whiteface.

• • •

They rose at four on the Saturday morning of
the show. They loaded the four horses into the
trailer and were on the road hauling in Beth's
old pickup by five. They watched the sun come
up from the highway into Detroit and stopped
for doughnuts at a truck stop filled with silent
truckdrivers warming hands around mugs of
coffee. Then they hit the highway once more.

At the show grounds, they unloaded the
horses and tied them to iron loops on the trailer.
Cora and two other students who would ride
for Beth showed up with nervous mothers. Then
began the laborious grooming. Not only must
the horses be shining and clean, their manes and
tails had to be braided with colored yarn, their
hooves polished. They all worked. Even two of

the mothers helped. The other mother paced and smoked.

A nervous Cora, grooming Cloud, began a litany of terrible falls at horse shows, ones she'd seen or read about. Faith shuddered at grisly accounts of broken necks over jumps, broken legs of horses and riders. She was delighted when Gem told Cora, "Stop polluting my space." After that Cora worked in abused silence.

The horses sensed the excitement in the preparations. The more elegant they began to look, the prouder they stood. Their nostrils widened and their eyes rolled back. After the horses were ready, Faith helped Gem put her hair in a French braid caught in a blue silk ribbon. Then Beth called her riders together to distribute the hunt caps. Gem grabbed quickly at a new cap of dark blue velvet. She crammed it on her head. Although it was too small for her French-braided hair, she insisted it fit fine.

Cinderella's sister, thought Faith smugly. She walked away from the group, suddenly lonely and missing Blackie Whiteface.

There were riders and trailers and horses all over the grounds. Faith wandered about, amazed at how many people wanted to risk their necks. The grass of the show ring was like a carpet and there were flowers crowded lavishly around all the jumps. Banners fluttered from the tall, white-painted judges' stand perched high beside the ring. Dressing up danger, thought Faith.

There were spectators sitting in bleachers and a well-dressed group under an awning at decorated tables. A good rider could earn points to ride in the big show at Madison Square Garden and events in Washington, D.C., and Pennsylvania. Faith felt a surprising tug of sympathetic terror for her sister, riding in such an important event.

But in the first two Equitation on the Flat classes, Gem took third-place yellow ribbons, while Faith gaped from the sidelines.

Then she was lonelier than ever and wandered off by the food tent. She waited in line for the hot, oozing sloppy joe sandwiches everyone seemed to be eating. Ahead of her stood a tall man in a cowboy hat. The way he stood reminded Faith of her father and she felt a rush of homesickness. She peered around the man to see what he looked like.

He had a blondish beard and smile lines at the corners of his eyes. His face didn't resemble her dad's at all. In his mouth was a toothpick. He smiled down into her face.

"What's doin', Red?" he asked her around the toothpick.

Faith was so pleased, she blushed.

"Looks like you been working hard." He nodded toward her dirty, straw-covered jeans. Faith blushed again and hid her hands behind her back. She knew her hands were grimy from grooming horses and her nails were black. Suddenly she realized she was going in to have lunch and she hadn't even remembered to wash her hands. That was a rule back home—clean hands or no meal. Beth, too, usually reminded them before eating.

"Excuse me," she whispered and fled from the line to search out the washroom.

Later, after she'd eaten her sloppy joe underneath a tree, she saw the cowboy leaning against the stairs by the judges' booth. She wandered over to him, drawn by his big worn hat and the easy way he stood. He was still chewing a toothpick. She wondered what he was doing at an English hunt-seat show. Cowboys didn't ride the same as English-trained riders. Even their saddles were different.

She leaned against the white rail of the ring, sighing as she looked at the preparations for the next class.

"You scare real easy, miss," remarked the cowboy. Faith's heart went cold. Who had told him she was a coward? But the cowboy added, "What did I say t'make you run off?"

Faith was so relieved she giggled. "Just went to wash up before lunch."

"You ride?" asked the cowboy, shifting his weight against the railing.

"I used to," replied Faith. That was at least half true. "But horses aren't my favorite thing." She waited for him to ask about her favorite thing. She would tell him about Blackie Whiteface or Rackity or the rabbits in her backyard at home.

But he drawled, "What're you doing here?" Faith looked up at him, hesitating. He smiled. "This is a heck of a place for somebody who's not into horses." His eyes were tan colored and warm. Like his skin and beard and his smooth, taffy-colored boots. She liked the soft way he spoke.

"I'm visiting," said Faith. "And I help with the horses." She nodded. "There's work for two or three at Beth's farm."

"Is that Beth?" asked the cowboy. He fanned his chin toward the line of horses and riders waiting outside the ring.

It was Beth, giving last-minute words to her riders, dark-honey hair straggling down out of her ponytail. She had her stall mucker boots on, which made her feet look like Beetle Bailey's in the comics. Her face was sweaty.

Faith realized he had been watching Beth for some time, not Gem, beautiful in her blue velvet hunt cap.

"That's Beth," she answered. "She's talking to my sister." Faith watched the cowboy's face. "My sister is a pretty good rider even though she just learned this summer. She still has to look down to check her leads, but Beth says she has a good chance to place. Beth says judges are biased."

The cowboy looked at her with interest. Encouraged, Faith went on. "Some judges don't like boy riders—or fat girls—or Appaloosa horses . . . no matter how good they are. Beth says most judges love thin, blond girls on big grays or blacks."

"Is that a fact," said the man. He switched his toothpick. "Probably so."

"The class my sister rides in won't be the real big jumps," she continued to inform him. "They change the course and raise the fences later for the real good riders."

"Yeah," he agreed.

Faith didn't usually talk at such a rate to strangers. But there was something about the cowboy, a kind of warm charge that seethed from his skin and clothing. And he liked her, she could tell.

He smiled around the toothpick, showing nice, strong, even teeth.

"Where do you live?" asked Faith.

"Oh, anywhere," he said, his eyes turning back

toward Beth. She was still talking to Gem, stroking Rambler's neck. "Everywhere."

Nowhere, I bet, thought Faith. A wandering cowboy. She edged nearer along the rail, drawn by his pleasantness, and looked up at his face.

"What do you do?" she asked.

He looked down at her, amused. "Are you nosy?" he teased, "or just careful? How many questions you gonna ask before I get to tell you my name, my age—and how much money I make?"

"How much money do you make?" asked Faith, delighted with her new sauciness. She saw herself flirting like Gem.

The cowboy spit out the toothpick, threw back his head and laughed.

"You're quite an ol' gal, Red." Faith smiled. The cowboy had a wonderful laugh. She noticed that his hands were fine, with very clean nails. Perhaps he was a movie cowboy. Most people who rode horses had tougher-looking hands. Who cared? A warm excitement fluttered in her throat.

She glanced hastily over at Beth, talking now to Cora, who sat on Cloud. Beth's hands were gentle on the neck of the big, black horse, stroking. Faith knew that Beth's nails were chipped and dirty, the palms callused. She tried to look at Beth through the cowboy's eyes and, for a brief instant, Beth came into focus as Faith had never seen her. Her serious face, intent upon her student, bloomed rich with color. There was a vast quiet beneath her hands against the dark horse. Her strong arms were smooth and tanned. Why, she's beautiful, thought Faith.

A flash of jealousy shriveled her briefly. Then she pushed it away, thinking, he's not going to wait till I grow up. But I could give him to Beth. *Like a carrot.* Maybe she'd be grateful. Maybe he'd visit a lot.

Then the loudspeaker interrupted her dreaming. They were calling the riders up for the next class. There was excitement along with dust rising in the air as horses and riders approached the ring.

"Gotta go," the cowboy said. He turned and mounted the ladder into the judges' booth. "See ya later, Red."

Surprised, she watched him enter the booth. Then, afraid of losing him, she called up, "What's your name?"

"Ben," he called back, "Ben Warren from Pennsylvania. Your Beth has heard my name before, I betcha."

Pennsylvania? Faith was disappointed. She had hoped for Montana or Wyoming.

But the real surprise came when she began to realize that Ben Warren was in the judges' booth because he was one of the judges.

Over the loudspeaker came the announcer's voice. "Afternoon, ladies and gentlemen. Most of you are already pretty familiar with our judge for the Equitation over Fences events. Mr. Ben Warren comes to us from Greenvalley, Pennsylvania . . ."

From below, Faith let this new knowledge sink in. The cowboy was a lot more than a cowboy. Then embarrassment came. What had she said to him—about judges being biased? And about her sister looking down for the right lead? Oh no! She had even explained to a *judge* about the raising of the fences.

In a hot glow of shame, she fixed her eyes on the activity in the ring. She was barely able to enjoy how well the first rider fenced. She couldn't appreciate the tremor in the spectators when Cora, the star rider, went off course, forgetting the correct order of jumps. Cloud still pranced and snorted eagerly under the tearful girl as she left the ring, disqualified.

The next horse refused a fence, sending the rider catapulting through the air to land on the far side of the jump. Faith was too preoccupied to even gasp.

Then the announcer called Gem's name and

number, and Faith was finally able to focus on the ring. Her sister rode beautifully, turning corners with confidence, eyes up over the fences, hands forward and light. Faith couldn't tell if she looked down for her lead as she rounded her turns. Rambler flew over each obstacle and Gem settled him back nicely for the next fence. There was a round of applause when the pretty girl trotted off, her back proud and straight.

When the winners were announced, Gem had earned a first-place ribbon for the event. Faith stopped hating herself for bad-mouthing judges to an actual judge. She wondered, briefly, about Mr. Ben Warren's choice. Her sister had certainly ridden as if she had years of experience under her narrow belt.

When the cowboy climbed down from the judges' booth, she accosted him. "Is my sister really that good?"

Ben Warren chuckled. "I must admit, Red, I'm a little partial to black or gray horses and lean riders. Don't have to be pretty, but they have got to move in harmony and the rider must not make mistakes."

"Can't fat riders ever win?" asked Faith, a little spite lifting her voice.

"If they don't make mistakes, sure," answered Ben Warren. "*And* if their weight doesn't hinder the horse." His eyes crinkled when he smiled at her. Faith dropped her head, embarrassed before his niceness.

"First-place ribbon probably would've gone to Cora Whats-'er-name if she hadn't gone off course. But, who knows. Your sister rode well. I caught her checking for her leads once or twice but she was the best in the Novice Ridden class. She earned her ribbon."

Faith looked back up into the cowboy's smile. He was the nicest man outside her father she had ever known.

"Can you cook?" she asked.

9

I invited someone to dinner tomorrow," said Faith to Beth on the long drive home. "Okay?"

It was growing dark and Beth's face was in shadow.

"Hope your friend likes pizza," said Beth tiredly. "I've got a lot of catching up to do. We shot the entire day today."

"He's bringing the whole dinner!" announced Faith triumphantly. "He can cook. He said just to set the table, have the wine glasses chilled and fill the water glasses two thirds full."

There was a long silence while Beth digested this news. Faith could feel the truck slow up almost imperceptibly. Then Beth asked tersely from the shadows, "Wine glasses? *Whom* did you ask, young lady?"

"The judge," said Faith slowly, savoring the interest she could feel coming from both Beth and her half-dozing sister. Next to her, Gem stirred and sat up.

"Mr. Ben Warren, the judge. The judge of the Novice Ridden Hunter class—and the Baby Green over Fences and . . ." She frowned in the effort to remember. "All the Novice Hunter division. I don't remember them all—but the whole last half of the show was judged by Mr. Ben Warren, the one in the cowboy hat."

The silence that grew in the cab of the truck was finally broken by Gem. "You've got to be kidding! He's gorgeous! I can't believe it." But she knew Faith wasn't kidding. "The fox in the cowboy hat?" Gem's voice grew shrill with excitement. "He looks like a country-and-western star!"

"How very interesting," commented Beth. But she no longer sounded so tired. Faith couldn't tell if she was pleased, but Gem certainly was. Her sister began to plan out loud what had to be done to prepare for Mr. Ben Warren.

"We've got to vacuum. Faith, you vacuum. I'll dust." She rambled on and on. Did Beth have a tablecloth, a real one—and napkins? They simply couldn't use paper napkins when they were having wine. And couldn't they have just a little wine—Gem and Faith? Faith's could be mostly water—but just for the show of it? They'd have to launder the towels. "And oh!" Gem squeaked. "The bathrooms!"

Faith smiled to herself in the growing darkness of the cab. Squeezed in between Gem and Beth, she remembered the cowboy's slow grin when she'd asked him if he cooked. He had offered to prove it. Then, made bold by his delight with her, Faith had brazenly suggested he come over the next day and fix Sunday dinner.

"How many?" he had asked. "How many eatin'?"

"Just me and my sister. We don't eat much. And Beth. She eats a lot."

He had laughed then and asked for the address. Faith could only remember the phone number of the farm. He pulled out a little gold pencil and a tiny notebook and wrote it down.

"Maybe he won't come," she said into the darkness of the cab, interrupting Gem's breathless planning. "He only has the phone number."

"Well, we'll see," said Beth calmly. "It's either a grand feast for four or pizza for three."

Both Faith and Gem groaned. The time had come at last for a change.

• • •

The next day, Faith was wakened by an insistent Gem, who was ignoring her beauty sleep for once.

"If we're going to get this place presentable, we'd better get started." Her voice was excited and driving. "Get up so we can make the bed."

Grumbling, Faith eased Blackie Whiteface to the floor. She would have to do her secret jogging later. She helped Gem shake the sheets up and make the bed.

"I want my breakfast," said Faith stoutly, more to resist Gem's bossiness than because she was hungry. Grudgingly she had to admire her sister's energy but Gem was taking over her idea— her gift. It was a bigger and better gift than being a blue-ribbon rider or a good weeder.

"How can you be hungry?" asked Gem. "I'm not hungry."

"He's not coming to see *you*," hissed Faith. "He doesn't even know you exist! *I* invited him. He's *my* friend. And he's coming to see Beth more than anyone." When she said this, it stung a little. She thought wistfully of the cowboy's smile and his fine hands.

Gem paused, looking hurt. Then she said, "He gave *me* a blue ribbon, so he must know I exist."

"Well, all you had to do to get a blue ribbon was to be blond and ride a gray horse, that's all," lashed Faith cruelly. "He *saw* you looking down!"

But her sister had recovered her composure. She said reasonably, "Come on. We've got to

straighten up the bathroom and the kitchen—
and find the wine glasses and real napkins." Faith
sourly acquiesced. Gem's plans were wonderful
embellishments on her own daring idea.

"Animals first," Beth reminded them. "It'll go
faster if we all help." She aimed the last remark
at Gem but looked surprised when Faith groaned
along with Gem.

"Even in emergencies?" Faith asked. She
wanted Beth to understand that she wasn't
shirking.

"Animals *are* the emergency," said Beth firmly.

So they spent the next hour feeding horses,
the donkey, sheep, dogs and cats. It took
another hour to medicate a kick wound on
Hobo's shoulder and knock a leaning fence post
back in.

Faith itched with impatience. Gem looked as
if she would explode.

Finally, farm chores finished, the girls at-
tacked the kitchen. It had served as a catchall
during the preparations for the show. Beth
seemed amused at their furious activity, but she
quietly picked up the living room and began to
run the vacuum.

"She's pretty laid-back for a prospective lover,"
whispered Gem to Faith. But later on, after Gem
had discovered linen napkins neatly tucked in
the back of a cupboard, Beth appeared with a

sturdy carton containing some beautiful crystal glasses that had been her grandmother's. There were seven wine glasses and six water goblets.

"I've never used these," she mused, taking them out of the straw they were packed in. She held one up to the window. The light leapt and shimmered like a shattered rainbow trapped inside the glass.

Oh, I hope he comes, thought Faith and, as if she had signaled Ben Warren, the phone rang. When Beth answered, it was the cowboy asking for directions.

After that, Beth disappeared upstairs to change her clothes. Faith and Gem stuffed the remaining clutter into the hall closet—sacks of cat food and kitty litter, looping reins of broken tack and a bag of unsorted laundry. The door would barely close and it took the two of them, throwing themselves against it, to finally latch it shut.

"If anyone knocks the doorknob, it'll explode," giggled Gem, which sent them both into a storm of laughter.

Then it was left to Faith to set the table with the mismatched silver and old flowered plates. She polished each plate as she set it down. She worried a little about Beth falling asleep right after dinner as she often did, sometimes nodding in her chair right at the table.

Gem disappeared, first into the bathroom to

rim her eyes with blue mascara. Then she scurried upstairs to put on her faded, skin-tight cutoffs, rearrange the stuffing in her bra and pull on a beautiful silk sweater. "The contrast will be smashing!" she had informed Faith.

Faith did not believe the contrast would be so smashing. But, she thought grudgingly, Gem will probably look beautiful anyway. For a moment she considered asking to borrow a blouse from her sister. But she was comfortable in her white T-shirt and her jeans were clean. She hoped Gem wouldn't outshine Beth—or the crystal glasses, either.

On a sudden inspiration, she ran outside to the garden to pick marigolds and daisies and a pretty blue-flower weed.

She was standing with an armload of flowers when the yellow van pulled into the long drive. She could see it slow down at the bridge and lurch up past the sheep field, a foreigner feeling his way in a new place.

It was a big van. She noticed that it was very clean, not like Beth's old truck or her dust-coated Horizon with its "I Brake for Animals" bumper sticker. He really can live anywhere, thought Faith. Delight at his coming flooded her.

The screen door banged but she barely noticed Gem come out, or Blackie Whiteface curling around her legs. Wolfie bounded barking to meet the visitor. Beth peered briefly from an upstairs window.

Faith waited, holding the flowers, feeling like a queen welcoming royalty from another country. The big yellow van pulled smoothly to a stop by the back porch.

"Hi, Red," said Ben Warren, sliding out of the driver's seat. He walked up and smiled down into her face. He wasn't wearing the toothpick. The wrinkles deepened warmly around his tan eyes. "You look like a bride with those flowers," he said, and smoothed his hand over the sheen of her red hair. "Mighty pretty."

Faith was so flushed with delight that she didn't even mind Gem posing on the back porch with her lion hair flung back. But then Beth came out of the door, and it wasn't any Beth she knew.

Faith had never seen Beth in a dress and hadn't known she even owned a pair of high heels. She looked uncomfortable and unsteady. The dress she wore was a faded yellow with drooping shoulders, cut simply, but somehow belonging to a half generation earlier. It had creases running across the skirt as if it had been folded a long time. The short sleeves were too tight around Beth's round arms. Her ponytail, now pulled to one side, gave her an unnaturally jaunty look.

After a frozen minute, Beth wobbled over to the porch steps. Her welcoming smile was drowned by the worry on her face.

She's worried about falling down the steps, realized Faith. Gem shot her a look of wide-eyed, exaggerated horror, which usually made Faith want to laugh. Now, it merely increased her discomfort. She wished fiercely that Beth would go inside and change back into her jeans.

To make matters worse, Ben Warren's face assumed a false look of heartiness. He strode up to where Beth stood and said in an uncomfortable voice, "This must be Beth."

"No, it isn't!" erupted Faith. "She usually looks much better!"

There was a shocked silence. Faith could hear the tail of her sister's gasp. And then Beth laughed. It was a big, deep laugh. She had come back among the living. She stopped wobbling and leaned against the old, peeling porch column. Her face relaxed and smiled.

"You were right, Ben Warren, yesterday when you told Faith I would know your name. I know you."

The genuine ease flooded back into the cowboy's manner. He chuckled, put one boot on the lower step and leaned into his knee.

"I sure know *you*, lady," he admitted. "You're

a legend. Turned down fifty thousand green ones for that fine black Thoroughbred of yours. That right?"

Beth looked startled and then blushed.

"I've watched you ride many a time," continued the cowboy. "Now I watch your students ride." He paused, then said softly, "The dynamite lady, Miss Beth Holbein. Pleased to meet you at last."

He smiled a real smile into her face. There was a kind of burning in the air between them, like electricity. Gem shot Faith a knowing look but Faith ignored it. They really like each other, she thought a trifle sadly. But she comforted herself that this was her gift to Beth, her cowboy.

• • •

They all helped Ben Warren carry bags of groceries into the newly cleaned kitchen. Faith steered him carefully past the hall closet. Then she arranged the flowers on the table, letting them spill and trail from an old milk pail.

It was a lovely evening, despite some minor setbacks. Beth's high heels menaced her walking. A sheep got loose and wandered around outside the house. Ben Warren had to sharpen the dull kitchen knives before he could begin cooking.

"Dull knives are dangerous knives," he said

as he slid the newly sharpened blade into a chicken breast, neatly severing the flesh from the rib bones. "You wind up forcing the blade and you can slip and cut yourself."

Faith watched, entranced. He arranged the chicken in a baking crock with tiny new potatoes and artichoke hearts. Faith had never liked artichokes much. But when she saw them, hot from the oven, nestled next to chicken and potatoes in a bubbly sauce, she could hardly wait until they sat down to eat.

Gem was allowed a half glass of wine and Faith had mineral water with a dash of wine. There were hot rolls. Beth had picked fresh lettuce from her garden to toss with tomatoes, sweet onions and Ben Warren's homemade dressing.

"Oh," breathed Faith as they all sat down and spread the napkins in their laps. "Oh . . ." A phrase of her grandfather's came to mind. "What a sumptuous repast!" she said.

They all clinked glasses while the escaped sheep peered through the dining room window.

• • •

The rest of the evening was wonderful, too. Beth took off her shoes and walked barefoot in her old-fashioned dress. She did not flirt like Gem flirted. She blushed and beamed. They all did the dishes. Ben Warren insisted. "You have to get this stuff over with or it just hangs on," he said.

Then he gave them a grand tour of his van. It was neat as a pin. Up front he had a tape deck and a citizens band radio. Behind the front seats was a little kitchen with a real sink, a stove and a miniature refrigerator. There was even a tiny bathroom with the towel and washcloth neatly in place. In a narrow closet hung his clothes, shirts all facing left. Faith thought of the hall closet back at the house and shuddered.

In the back of the van was a bunk bed on which sat a guitar. Faith was rapt when Ben Warren picked it up and began to hum.

He played "Harvest Moon" and they all sang. He played "The Ash Grove." Then Gem sang "I'm Bidin' My Time" in her very beautiful, clear soprano voice and Faith hated her only briefly.

Faith had never seen Beth smile so much. Nor had she ever seen her so wide awake at this hour of the evening unless there was an emergency with a sick horse or a broken water pump. Tonight Beth's eyes were bright and merry. She didn't seem the least bit tired. Nobody, in fact, was tired, and it was midnight before anyone realized how late it was.

Smiling, Beth suggested that it was time to "hit the hay, girls." Faith and Gem went reluctantly up to their bedroom, but they left the stairwell door open a crack. After they had changed into their nightclothes, they crept back down the stairway, smothering giggles, and crouched near the bottom, trying to hear what Beth and Ben were saying to each other in the living room.

Blackie Whiteface came tumbling down the stairs, his toenails clicking against the wooden steps. Faith hushed him and he curled up in her lap, licking her fingers.

Bored by the long pauses between the soft conversation in the living room, Faith fell asleep in the stairwell, leaning against her sister. She was startled awake as she and Gem and Blackie Whiteface rolled, bumpity-thump, down the last couple of steps and thudded into the stairwell door. They had all dropped asleep against each other and collapsed like a house of cards. Ben Warren, who had leaped to his feet at the crash of bodies, ran to the door and yanked it open. It was not the door to the stairwell, but the hall closet door.

There was a clatter and thump and the cowboy's shout of alarm. When the girls peeked around the doorjamb, they saw an amazed Ben Warren covered with loops of tack, dirty laundry and kitty litter. Beth was leaning against a wall, her hand over her mouth. Faith couldn't tell whether she was laughing or just plain mortified.

"Well," said Ben Warren, waving his arms to disentangle himself. Then he saw the sisters and a frightened kitten peering from behind the door and began to laugh. "You sure need some organizing around here," was all he said.

10

*F*aith was so high on the overwhelming success of the dinner party that she floated about
for a week, absorbed by Beth and Ben's interest
in each other.

When Ben Warren wasn't off judging a horse
show, he lived in his van parked next to the
garden. There was a new atmosphere about the
place.

Beth was warm with Faith these days and
smiled often. She was amused that Ben Warren
had cleaned up her kitchen spick and span and
she couldn't find anything anymore. He had even
straightened up Beth's closet, and all her shirts
and blouses were now facing left.

The cowboy had begun to finish up the sheep's
bathroom, too. In the evenings, he and Beth

talked over where the new shelving would go and whether the shower should be separate from the tub.

Faith basked in her own virtues. She whistled as she shoved damp clothes into the dryer. She hummed as she did the dishes. Ben Warren called her Cinderella, but she could tell he admired her sense of order. Once he watched her lunge a horse in the ring. She showed off by calling for a canter, something she was still reluctant to do, and then she brought the swift-moving animal back down to a smooth trot. Ben Warren tipped his hat to her. "Pretty good stuff," he said. Sometimes the world is wonderful, thought Faith.

One morning, in the tilting mirror of their bedroom, Faith was startled out of her happy satisfaction. Something had happened to her thighs. At first, she was horrified. I'm going to have a bulge in my thighs, she thought. I'm growing up into a person with bulging thighs. Her calves, she noticed, were rounded out too. She decided against the striped shorts she had pulled from the drawer. Instead she dragged on a pair of dirty jeans.

It seemed impossible that her tiptoe jogging in the morning could be responsible for the new shape of her legs. Nor could the hamstring toe-walk up the stairs at night. True, she did her exercises easily and automatically. She now jogged five minutes in place without breathing heavily.

Faith was desperate to wake her sister and discuss her legs. But she knew Gem would be impossible to talk to this early. Later, she thought, she would ask Gem about her thighs. Her sister had definite opinions about beauty. She was somehow always mysteriously aware of the right "look" in a person. "That's a cool jacket," she would whisper to Faith, nudging her. Or, "Did you see his *hair*cut? It's *atro*cious! He looks like a fish."

Faith ran downstairs and into the kitchen. Beth was already outside, feeding stock. Ben Warren's van was gone. The cowboy had a show to judge in Indiana. A few flies buzzed by the window and Faith swatted one out of existence with the swatter. Now that Ben Warren had repaired the screen doors there were only a few flies in the house.

Faith ate some cereal and carefully washed up her dishes, putting them away on the newly lined shelves. Gem would be getting up soon. She never slept past a riding lesson but she was often late to help Faith with the grooming.

Faith did most of the grooming and tacking up for the beginners' class. Beth had a lot of new students too small to do it themselves. The broad backs of horses seemed easier to reach with the brush these days.

On some mornings she actually enjoyed being close to the horses, slipping underneath their heavy necks to get to the other side. She could bridle them all now, wiggling her thumb and fingers into the sides of their mouths until they took the bit. Then she would spray them with fly spray and help the little ones mount.

Often she watched the lessons with a careful eye, listening to Beth's directions, looking to see if the riders followed them. She checked to see if she could "see daylight" between their knees and the saddle. New riders' knees always stuck out. The relief she had once felt at the beginning of each lesson—relief *not* to be riding—had been replaced by a vague envy.

The morning of her new-shaped legs, Faith left the kitchen with a firm purpose, ignoring the chill that cooled her heart. For several days she had been contemplating a daring move. Today, she thought, maybe I'll do it. Just sit on one of the horses when I bring him down to the ring. Just sit in the saddle. The chill moved into her middle.

She bounded from the porch, scattering a few barn cats. Cars were pulling in with students. She met Beth leading Rambler toward the stable.

"Good morning, lazybones," greeted Beth with a mild smile. "I've already tacked up Vixen and Hobo. I'll need Rambler here and the other four regulars. They're in the stalls." She handed the gray's lead rope to Faith. "You look ready for anything today."

"I am," said Faith, and led Rambler off. He went easily into his stall.

She was a little nervous tacking Harold up. Flies had invaded the stable and all the animals were jumpy. But she led the big bay outside to a stump and mounted easily. On the way down to the ring, from the high vista of his back, she felt such a rush of excitement and power that Harold surged momentarily into a trot. The old panic returned. She sat back and pulled him down into a walk, heaving a great breath. "Don't you dare, Harold," she muttered

Beth was in the ring with students when Faith rode Harold up. When she turned to take the horse from Faith, her eyebrows lifted. "What have we here?" was all she said.

Faith swung out of the saddle and slid down Harold's warm side to the ground. She handed the reins to Beth, trying to appear casual. "I'll ride all the others down." She ran back to the barn, flinging a friendly wave at the gathered mothers. Her back felt loose and strong and she wondered briefly how tall she had grown this summer.

But when she was grooming a restless Hobo, pestered by flies, he stepped on her once. Then, when she slapped his rump, he dangerously waved his hind leg. Cautiously she led him down to the ring, limping as she went, her foot smarting. "He's in a rotten mood today," she informed Beth.

She changed her mind about riding the others down. But later, Faith bragged to Brady in the barn that she had "taken up riding again." Brady just grunted and kept right on working. Faith realized she would have to look elsewhere for proper appreciation. In a way, she suspected she had told a lie to Brady. She wasn't sure she'd try riding a horse to the ring again.

But, several days later, she delivered first Harold, then Vixen by riding them down to the ring. She felt that, one of these days, she would take on Hobo, too.

The muscle roundness in Faith's calves and thighs didn't astonish Gem. When asked, she said, "Well, it looks like you're going to have *legs* after all, not those pale sticks you've been walking around on." It wasn't a whole lot of comfort. Still, Faith felt able to wear her shorts again, even though they were a little tight in the leg.

• • •

One evening, after the dishes were done and Ben Warren was cleaning his fingernails, he suggested to Beth that they go out dancing. "Found a nice place, Lady Beth, with some good music. It'll be somethin' new."

Gem looked up with interest. "A disco?" she asked. Ben laughed.

Beth was standing by the kitchen table cleaning tack. "I don't have time for *new*," she said impatiently. "Or discos." But then she joked, "I've got six more of these to do. If you want something new—here, clean some tack." She tossed a bridle at him. There was a long dead pause.

She meant it to be funny, thought Faith. Into the silence between the couple, Faith dropped an uneasy laugh. Then, quickly, she offered, "I'll do it, Beth." She grabbed the bridle from Ben's lap. "This is Cinderella's job." But Ben Warren did not smile. He got up and left the room, saying, "See you later." They heard the van start up and drive off.

Beth stopped rubbing oil into the bridle looped

over a chair. Gem paused in her perpetual nail polishing. Faith felt the air lie heavily on them, gathered about a table full of tack.

Gem finally shrugged and said, "I guess the honeymoon is over."

"No!" said Faith. When Gem and Beth looked at her in surprise she mumbled, "Honeymoons last two weeks. It's only been eleven days."

After that, small arguments constantly erupted between Beth and Ben. They were about trivial things. "If you put your blouse back the same way you took it out, your closet would stay neat," Ben would protest.

At first, Beth nodded and smiled, chiding him, calling him "Mr. Perfection." He called her "Willie Workhorse." Gradually, Beth stopped smiling and began to frown whenever the cowboy protested the way she did things.

Faith didn't understand it. Couldn't they tell when they would irritate each other? Couldn't they take the same kind of care with one another they had at first? In the beginning it had amused Ben that Beth went out of her way to use dirt roads instead of the nearby blacktop and highway. Now he criticized how dirty her car got. "Take the highway," he told her. "You're always late for things."

Now, during lessons and chores, Beth appeared distant, preoccupied. She didn't seem to notice Faith's increased efficiency with horses, how easily she groomed them.

"I call for a canter all the time now," Faith told Beth one afternoon as they brought in horses to be lunged.

"Good," said Beth—but she didn't seem to have heard.

Gem didn't appear worried about Beth and Ben when Faith tried to voice her distress. She was more concerned about when Owen was going to call next.

Gradually the arguments between Beth and Ben Warren became more intense. Bewildered, Faith gave up trying to intervene. The perfect relationship seemed to have turned upside down.

One afternoon, the cowboy stormed out of the house and into his van. He drove off in a fury of dust and spitting gravel, his van narrowly missing the corner of the bridge.

The atmosphere inside the house was grim. Beth sat in the kitchen cleaning another bridle with a cold, determined expression on her face. Faith felt defeated and lonely. She left to seek the quiet comfort of the barn, hoping Blackie Whiteface would be there. She wanted to cuddle him and nuzzle into the fur behind his neck. It always made her feel good.

She called his name into the barn loft. "Blackie? Blackie Whiteface? Hey!" He usually skittered out when he heard her voice. But he was not in the barn. Faith wandered down to the sheep pen. There was a bristling commotion in the ram section where two rams were challenging each other. Beth and Ben, thought Faith. Stubborn. Plain bullheaded.

Blackie Whiteface was there, perched atop the railing of the sheep pen watching the rams. His little white face peered down into the activity. He leaned so far forward into the pen he appeared to be glued by his hind feet to the top rail. The fury in the pen increased, raising dust. There was the thud of heads and horns, a jostling of woolly bodies.

"Blackie, get away from there," scolded Faith. The rams backed off from each other and lowered their heads. Their mean little eyes grew smaller.

Their charge was furious. They lurched. When they hit, their bodies plowed into the fence. Horns locked.

"Blackie!"

She cried out as the kitten was knocked from his perch. He fell like a stone into the pen—into the angry, blind activity between the rams.

Then she was screaming, "Blackie! Blackie!" She struggled over the fence, waving her arms at the rams. They backed off in astonishment at the power of her fury.

His little body lay in a crumpled heap. Faith knelt and touched the sprawled ball of fur. He was alive, his breathing slight.

Very gently, she eased her hands beneath the little form. With great care, she walked with him to the back porch. She sat down on the steps and cradled the warm little body in her lap. Blackie Whiteface mewed faintly and tried to lick her hand. She could feel his heartbeat through her palms . . . so faint. *Beat, beat,* and a long pause.

"Blackie? Blackie Whiteface?" she whispered. *Beat, beat.*

She knew when he left her. The beat was so faint, she held her breath. And then it was gone.

• • •

They planned a funeral for Blackie Whiteface. Beth lined an old shoebox with soft flannel. "We just want to ease him gently back into the cycle of life," said Beth. "Soon he'll be back in circulation again." She smiled sadly. "Part of a flower here, part of a tree . . . grass . . . part of a horse, part of you and part of me."

Faith was numb with misery. She didn't want a flower or a tree. She wanted the little black-and-white kitten who had slept curled against her every night.

Ben Warren returned in the late afternoon in

time to help dig the narrow little grave. They buried Blackie Whiteface near the woods under a big old hickory tree.

In the evening Ben held Faith in his lap as if she were a baby again. Faith leaned into his clean-smelling shoulder and let herself be that baby for a while.

Beth and Ben were gentle with each other too, speaking in soft, low voices. Gem held Faith's hand and offered to sing her any song she wanted to hear.

"Just hum," said Faith. "I think I'd like some humming." So Gem hummed *Ave Maria*, getting only a little carried away on the high notes. It was a very good evening in a way. When she went to bed, Faith plunged into sleep immediately and slept deeply all night.

• • •

The next day it was sunny and warm and seemed too bright. Faith's body felt heavy and slow. She went through the motions—cleaning up the dishes after breakfast, bringing the horses in for Beth's classes and helping groom and tack them up. There was not even the luster of fear around the horses anymore. She poked at her food at lunchtime; Ben's succulent meals didn't tempt her. She avoided the sheep and kept out of the barn loft where the mother and sisters of Blackie Whiteface romped and fought.

She wondered listlessly if the rest of her life would drag on this way, colorless and dull.

In the late afternoon, she plodded down to one of the horse fields. Gone was the sharp edge of anxiety she had always felt approaching it. She could hardly believe she had ever been that scared of anything, had *cared* that much.

She sat on the top rail of the fence in the warm sun. Horses grazed, switching at flies. She stared off over the fields and the strangest feeling came over her. She saw the sunlit fields as if through a gray veil. She felt them fading from her, everything slipping away, no longer hers. An emptiness invaded her, so terrible that she clutched the rail beneath her.

"Why so quiet, Red?" asked a voice near her elbow. Ben Warren leaned against the rail next to where she sat. She could not answer. His voice came to her through the grayness.

Then he reached his big, neat hand gently to the top of her head and smoothed her hair.

The awful emptiness welled up.

"I don't want to die," whispered Faith. The hum of insects came muffled through the veil.

"Who says you have to?" asked Ben Warren.

"Everybody dies," said Faith dully. But she

looked into his face near her shoulder. She felt the faint stirrings of hope.

"You won't die, Red," said Ben Warren. He tucked his finger under her chin and turned her face to his.

"Sometime, a long, long time from now, so far away neither of us can believe in it, a real old lady with your name and lots of memories you don't even have yet will die. But she won't mind."

He spoke slowly. "She'll be going on a new adventure, one you can't go on until you die— and she'll be ready. You can't go there until you're ready."

"Was Blackie Whiteface ready?" asked Faith, pulling away suspiciously. With the suspicion came a sharp bite of pain.

"I suspect he was," said Ben Warren. "It's just that you weren't ready for him to leave, is all."

"No," said Faith softly. "I wasn't."

Then Ben Warren hugged her again, quick and short, lifted her in one sweep from the fence and spanked her lightly on her bottom.

"Come on, Red," he said. "We gotta feed livestock."

Dutifully she followed him back to the barn, her gaze fixed on the taffy-colored boots and the grass slowly lifting back from his big footsteps.

∙ ∙ ∙

That night, lying next to her sleeping sister, Faith stared into the darkness of their room. The hollow by her shoulder where her kitten had curled every night felt cold. I don't have to worry about rolling on him, thought Faith. With that freedom came the memory of his little round belly, breathing in and out as he slept.

Tears ran silently from her eyes and into the hair by her ears. She lay that way for a long time, shaking with silent sobs, curbing her misery to keep from waking her sister. She stared into the room half the night and finally drifted into a choppy sleep filled with shards of dreams. She dreamed Blackie Whiteface was still alive and scratching on the screen door wanting to be let in.

Toward dawn she fell deeply, dreamlessly asleep. They let her sleep late. She woke up several times during the morning, then finally sat up. She found it odd that sunlight was pouring into the room, slanting bright and yellow across the floorboards. She climbed out of bed and went to the window.

In the fields below, horses grazed. She could hear the faint clatter from the kitchen where Ben Warren was washing dishes. Gem's trill of composed laughter told Faith her sister was on the telephone with Owen. Down by the barn, Beth emerged carrying grain for the stallion. The world was turning and turning. Faith leaned her head against the cool glass of the upper window.

The faint clean smell of outdoor horses and sun-warmed grass drifted past her face. She stretched her arms to the top of the window frame and took a deep breath.

She was growing hungry, but she wanted to wait a little before she stepped back into the world.

11

Late in August, the weather in lower Michigan was perfect. Occasional brief rainstorms kept the meadows lush. Although the flies persisted, the nights were now cold enough to kill off some of the pesky insects.

Tomatoes and zucchini reached their peak in the garden. Faith helped Beth harvest them both. Beth made vats of tomato sauce and they all ate zucchini forty different ways.

The loss of Blackie Whiteface made Faith more quiet and thoughtful than before. She fell back into the routine of the farm, but fragments of the kitten's lively spirit came to her at unexpected moments. When she went with Beth to bring in horses, her mind would fly unbidden to the big old hickory tree by the woods. She welcomed her tears at these times but went off by herself to shed them. Once, alone with Cloud, she dropped her brush and wept loudly against his warm neck.

The horses were in peak shape, despite the daily torment of the flies. Their coats gleamed with health and cleanness. They frolicked in their fields. They wandered from fly-switching groups to graze.

Watching them from her quietness, Faith saw the horses with a different awareness. She saw how they spoke with movement and stance, arguing and challenging. They raced. They scratched one another. They stood close, inhaling information. She watched them tease and nip each other. She was surprised their speech hadn't been clear to her before.

The stream of life at the farm gathered Faith in. One Saturday, a crew of neighbors came over in the morning for a tree felling. All morning Faith's ears were filled with the angry buzz of power saws. Four huge, dead oaks at one end of the biggest field were cut down. Great limbs were trimmed off, cut and stacked for winter firewood. Then Faith watched the crew wrap chains about the giant trunks and haul them with a tractor into the middle of the field.

In the stillness of the afternoon, they piled brush heavily about the trunks. Faith helped stuff newspapers inside the branches. Then Ben Warren touched a match to one of the crumpled newspapers and stood back. The newspaper flared up. The dry wood caught and leapt into flame. Like a neon decoration the flames ran along the trunk. The people standing about clapped and cheered as the twigs crackled wildly.

All afternoon they fed the fire, until finally the old, dried-out trunks caught. The flames settled into the crumbly wood of the great prone trees and glowed there, burning slowly.

That night, the slow fire lit up the field. The neighbors gathered there. They cooked thick steaks, speared and held over the fire with green branches. They toasted slabs of Ben Warren's homemade bread on long forks and slapped them onto cardboard plates to soak up the juices. There were ice hampers filled with lemonade and beer.

They toasted fat, dusty marshmallows, burning the skins crisp over their oozing insides, and ate them pressed in between melting chocolate graham crackers.

Ben Warren got out his guitar and played a rousing song. With sticky faces, everyone sang, wiping hands on their wads of gummy napkins.

Then Ben struck a mellow sweet chord and played a song no one had ever heard before "About this gal I know," he explained.

Faith knew it was Beth he was singing about,

although Ben didn't look at her right away. He sang about her smooth strong arms and her little waist.

Faith glanced hastily at Beth to see if she was listening, but Beth's face was in shadow. Faith couldn't see her expression.

> *And she can't lie—that gal o' mine,*
> *and a promise she will keep.*
> *She's honest as the day is long*
> *and stubborn as her sheep.*

There was clapping and some good-natured ribbing from the people gathered there. Beth's face moved out of the shadows into the glow from the fire. Faith could see she was smiling in a funny, shy way.

The heat of the fire held them all together in its slow burning. Now the great logs seemed lit from inside, their outer shape held together by the glow within. Like long lanterns on some strange planet, Faith thought, and we are travelers, unafraid.

The night was very black and clear, no moon but crisp stars. Everyone lay on blankets, talking quietly. Gem sat with Owen on a blanket. They held hands. Faith lay, sleepy, with her head in Beth's lap while Ben Warren smoothed her hair. She thought of Blackie Whiteface for the first time without the yawning ache. There seemed to be no loneliness or sadness anywhere in the world.

• • •

Problems aren't solved by one magical night, thought Faith several days later. It had been raining, off and on, all morning. There were puddles around the back porch and Wolfie had tracked mud all over the kitchen floor. Thunder rumble still hung in the sky, now near, now distant.

Beth couldn't teach on a rainy day, but she had been exercising horses in between thundershowers since breakfast. "They're getting sloppy from being ridden by too many novices," she explained when Faith questioned the purpose. "They need to be shaped up." And out she strode before it could rain again. Faith recognized the determined expression on her face. It meant: *Stay out of my way; there's too much to do!*

Faith sensed something stormy in the air besides the weather, but she couldn't put her finger on it.

That afternoon, Faith had just started clearing off the lunch dishes when Beth and Ben began one of their arguments. Faith could hear their voices in the living room. Their quarreling was easier for Faith to take when her sister was around, but Gem had gone off for a drive with

Owen and his mother. Owen was practicing for his driving test. Even Brady was gone, visiting family in Ohio.

Faith sighed. She could tell this argument was going to be a long one. Beth had lost several phone bills somewhere among her scattered mail and forgotten to pay them. Now the phone line had been disconnected. Ben Warren couldn't make some calls about a horse show in Canada. The quarrel, which had started with Beth's messy desk, had progressed to the messy condition of her closets.

"Lady, I can't function in chaos," the cowboy was saying. His nice, soft tones were gone. Gone the slow drawl.

Beth muttered something about having horses to exercise. Ben interrupted. "*You* can't function in it either, by the looks of things," he said. "All those emergencies of yours are your own doing."

"I do all right." Beth raised her voice, cold as the edge of a knife. "I *function* best without interference."

A terrible silence. Then Beth continued, slow and stubborn. "While you are lining up boots and organizing bills, horses get out and run all up and down the road—or the donkey eats up half my garden or a sheep drowns! What good are boots in a row while horses are waiting to be exercised? Or when my sheep is struggling to get out of a water tub?"

That's not Ben Warren's fault, objected Faith.

"Proving my point," roared Ben Warren. "Anybody with just a tad more brains than a sheep knows enough not to sink a watering tub in the same field with them!"

They're not being fair. Not fair. Faith tuned out the voices, running the water full blast in the kitchen sink, churning up the suds. She scrubbed furiously at a frying pan.

Then she realized it was quiet in the living room. She couldn't stand it and slipped into the doorway to have a look.

Ben Warren sat on a stool by the old-fashioned desk. His shoulders were slumped forward. "What's the use," he said quietly.

Beth was at the window, looking out. Her face was closed and pale.

"What's the point?" He wasn't really asking a question.

It wasn't the usual argument after all. It wasn't slam-the-door anger where Ben Warren stalked off forgetting his cowboy hat, leaving everything behind in his angry dust. And came back later for it. And made up.

This was cold, quiet, giving-up anger. The cowboy got up from the stool. Slowly he went from room to room gathering his belongings. He didn't forget his socks and his blue work shirts in the laundry basket—or his toothpicks or the special coffee cup over the sink. It didn't take him long. He had most of his stuff in his van anyway, neatly hanging or filed away.

"You can keep the food in the freezer," he said quietly to Beth. He was stuffing things into a blue denim bag. Beth still stood by the window looking out, a statue with fists chenched, face of stone.

She didn't turn. Faith felt a rush of despair. Ben Warren smiled wanly at her as he opened the screen door. " 'Bye, Red," he said. He didn't even slam the screen door when he left.

Faith ran out behind him, tagging after his heels. He swung himself in the side door of the yellow van.

"Ben?" asked Faith.

He turned and looked down at her from the doorway.

"You coming back?"

"Don't think so, Red." His drawl was heavy and serious.

"Can I write you a letter? Someplace?" asked Faith. "Do you have an address? Anywhere else, I mean?"

"I'll send you a card when I get somewhere." He looked at her for a moment. Faith felt tears coming on. Then he said, "Don't make it harder, Red." He turned, closing the van door gently behind him.

"It's going to rain," Faith said to the closed door.

She waited for the van to pull out. He must be putting things away, she thought. Even when he's mad, he's neat.

Then she turned and ran back to the house. Beth wasn't in the living room anymore. Or the kitchen. Faith hurried, calling through the house, "Beth! Beth!" No answer from upstairs either. She felt meanness spreading through her body.

"Don't you like Ben Warren?" she wanted to ask her. *My cowboy? I gave him to you. Is that what you do with a present?*

She slammed out onto the porch. The van was still there. Then she saw Beth striding down to the barn. She's just going to keep on working, thought Faith.

She watched Beth disappear into the stable and then reappear, lugging a saddle and with a bridle over her shoulder.

From the distant sky, a faint rumble of thunder seemed ridiculously appropriate. Up to the rain-green field strode Beth, hardly slowed by the weight of the saddle.

Nothing stops her, thought Faith in dismay. Beth hoisted the tack onto the fence rail and marched into the field. Faith watched her catch Cloud without so much as a greeting or a pretty please.

She's already exercised Cloud, thought Faith, and then remembered how Beth had ridden out her sorrow when Shinyface was sold.

Dark clouds were re-forming overhead and the low rumble of thunder growled nearer. Faith felt a fresh surge of anger. They would all have to sit around oiling down wet tack tonight so it wouldn't stiffen from being rained on. And if somebody didn't do something, Ben wouldn't even be there, his easy presence warming the room. She'd have to make Beth see. She jumped off the porch and began to run down to the gate. Beth had finished tacking up Cloud by the fence.

"It's going to rain, Beth," hollered Faith, hoping to make her pause. But Beth swung neatly up into the saddle. She turned the big black horse and trotted past Faith, leaving a wake like electricity. Off across the big wet field they went. Faith watched her fall into the quick rhythm of the horse, her honey-dark ponytail bobbing in time with Cloud's tail. The long motion of her back as she posted up and down was easy and sure, as smooth as breathing. Over the crest of the hill they disappeared, heading toward the woods.

"You can clean up your tack by yourself!" Faith shouted after her.

She looked back and Ben Warren's van was still in the driveway. She had the feeling he was waiting in there, not wanting to leave. If she could just get Beth to stop for a minute.

She crawled through the fence and began to run across the wet field. Grass soaked her sneakers. Her feet sank into the soft earth. It took ages to reach the top of the hill. Once there, she paused to catch her breath and get her bearings.

She could see Beth and the black horse, dwarfed by distance. Thunder rumbled again and Beth leaned to pat Cloud's neck. Faith could almost hear the soothing, "Okay, sweet boy— okay."

Beth eased Cloud into a canter and he moved out faster and faster, until they were flying toward the woods.

How beautiful she is, thought Faith. The half-light of the approaching rain cast no shadows. Everything stood out clearly, the blades of grass, the perfect miniature of horse and rider against the darkened trees. Ben should see her, Faith thought. He wouldn't be able to leave.

Even the small brown rabbit showed clearly, and Faith saw him with pleasure. Her animal-person eyes caught the movement as he darted out of the brush, startled by the activity in the field. His little body plunged in a zigzag pattern into the path of the thundering horse.

Faith cried out. Cloud stopped short. He spun up and around. Beth hurtled from his back, somersaulting through the air. Faith heard her land with a muffled crunch. The crumpled figure twitched against a rubble of wood and stones. Then she lay still.

Faith was running before she knew it. Then she stopped, half-turned toward the house. Shouted, "Ben! Ben!"

No sign of life about the van. Wolfie lay by the back porch. She cupped her hands at her mouth. Yelled at the top of her lungs, "BEN! HELP! BEHHHHHNN!" Nothing stirred except Wolfie. He got up, stretched and yawned.

Faith whirled about and ran again toward Beth. When she reached the fallen figure, she was out of breath. Beth lay half on her side. One arm twisted oddly beneath her. Her face had no color. Protruding from her torn shirt by the collar was what Faith at first took to be the handle of something—a screwdriver—grayish with a jagged end Then a bleat of fear slipped from Faith's lips. It was a bone. A little circle of blood stained the shirt collar. The bone glistened wetly.

Had Ben heard her call? Where was he? She

had a momentary vision of him folding a T-shirt and closing a drawer.

Faith knelt down in the rubble and put her head carefully against Beth's chest. She could hear the healthy thud of Beth's heart.

She stood up and looked back toward the distant driveway. Her own heart skipped a beat. The yellow van was disappearing, the *purrumble* of its motor thinning out as it got farther down the drive. She hadn't even heard it start.

"Oh, *no!*" she groaned. She moved to run toward the van, the house, the phone. And caught herself. Wasted motion. Too late. No Ben. No phone.

The nearest neighbors were too far away. Lightning flashed a jagged opening down the sky. A terrible helplessness seized her, and the old, familiar smallness. She heard herself moan a long whimpering sound. At the same time, questions whirled in her head.

How long would it take Ben Warren to reach the highway? How much time? Could she cut him off some way?

She felt a tug at her sleeve and turned in panic. It was Cloud, looking contrite. He nosed her shoulder.

"Oh, Cloud," she breathed, and the helplessness dissolved. She straightened his reins. Her eyes scanned the distance where fencerow trees thinned out. Beyond the next field and meadow was a faraway blacktop road. It was Ben Warren's usual route from the farm and connected with the highway. He would be at the bridge now. A minute or two and he would reach the dirt road. He still had to drive past Beth's big sheep fields and an abandoned farm before he turned onto the blacktop.

"Stay there!" she commanded Cloud. She ran to Beth's half dismantled mower and yanked off the tarp covering it. She dragged the tarp across the grass to Beth. Gently she spread it over the prone body, making a little tent over her face. Beth moaned but did not move or awaken.

Faith hurried back to Cloud and straightened out his stirrup irons. She guessed at the correct length and pulled them up three notches to fit her legs. Then she led the horse to a great rock where she could stand and hoist herself into the saddle. Her sneakers squished in the irons and her feet felt heavy. The stirrups were still too long, but Beth moaned again. There wasn't time to fumble with buckles.

In Faith's mind was forming the only plan she could think of. She would have to be quick and cut across Beth's two fields and then across the neighbor's meadow. She just might cut off Ben Warren's van before it turned from the blacktop onto the highway.

Lightning flashed again with an accompanying roll of thunder. Cloud's ears shot forward. Faith could hear the quick breath that signaled the big horse's panic. "Easy," she said. She stroked his neck. In quieting the big animal, she felt herself grow calm. Now. She turned him and pressed her legs into his sides.

Cloud lurched into a frightened canter, unsteady. Fear and the familiar wobble returned to chill Faith briefly. Then she sat back and gave a light tug on the reins. "Easy, Cloud," she said. She could feel him relax. She patted his neck. "Easy." She guided him toward the line of trees that marked a long-gone fence.

Now Cloud settled into a swift, light canter, comforted by Faith's voice and the direction from her legs. It's not all that far, she kept thinking to herself.

It began to rain, heavy and sudden, big drops. Before they crossed over into Beth's next field, horse and rider were both drenched. Faith could not see, through the curtain of rain, any sign of Ben Warren's van.

She leaned forward now and urged Cloud into a gallop. Across the field they flew, swallowing up the wet ground. No holes, she prayed, no holes, please. Briefly, the brown rabbit slipped in and out of her mind. Rain stung her eyes, blinding her. All the stray ends of her panic joined with the force of the great horse into a strange excitement. *So this is how it feels.*

She marked her direction now, eyes squinted against the arrows of rain, by the dim outline of a white shed in the distance. Ben Warren would have to turn at that point.

As she neared the end of the field, she suddenly noticed the wooden fence. Now she remembered. It separated Beth's field from the neighbor's meadow. No quick way around. She knew she would have to jump.

Into her mind came the several commands Beth shouted most in her jumping classes. "Hands forward. Eyes up. Grab mane! Ask him! With your legs. *Ask* him!"

It was too late to stop and there was no time to think. She aimed Cloud at the fence. Could he see it through the downpour? The rain whipped at her face. The pounding of hooves filled her ears. The fence seemed to come at them. Cloud's powerful body gathered beneath her and she moved her hands forward. She raised her eyes into the stinging rain, into the drenched meadow beyond. She asked him. With a great surge, Cloud soared over the fence and landed with a satisfied snort on the other side. A yelp of alarm escaped from Faith. She felt herself slipping from the saddle. *"Sit up! Don't fall!"* said Beth in her mind. She struggled back into the wet seat. It took her several gasping seconds to settle Cloud down and find his rhythm again.

The blacktop road, a short distance beyond the white shed, was empty. The image of the bloody bone protruding from Beth's shirt grabbed her mind. She pressed Cloud through her sodden pant legs. They tore across the meadow and then alongside the blacktop. The curve ahead told Faith nothing. But when they reached and rounded it, she could see, not far away, Ben Warren's van slowing down for the highway access road.

"Ben!" she yelled. "Ben!" Cloud sensed the urgency and pressed on faster.

"Ben, WAIT!" The van turned onto the access road.

No! She was losing him. The yellow van, wheels spattering along the wet surface, began to speed up to join the highway traffic.

"Ben! BEN!" Cloud's hooves clattered on the blacktop. They were too far away. She stayed to the left behind the van, praying Ben would check his rearview mirror.

And he must have. Gradually, because of the slick pavement, Ben Warren slowed down.

And stopped. The van's hazard lights went on, blinking dimly through the rain. Horse and rider raced toward the blurry shape.

As long as she lived, Faith would remember

the look of astonishment on Ben Warren's face through the rain-spotted window.

• • •

Faith took the road home, a good mile longer. "Dangerous to fence in this downpour," Ben Warren had warned her as he pulled out for the farm. He had used the emergency frequency on his CB to call the rescue squad.

The rain turned to a light drizzle. The memory of Beth's sturdy heartbeat softened Faith's concern and mingled with her relief that the cowboy was back.

Cloud trotted smoothly, spattering wet pebbles. A surge of elation filled Faith and she laughed out loud, lifting her face into the wet sprinkle. *What have I done?* She thought of the fence blurred by rain, Cloud's pounding hooves. Perhaps this was how Gem felt when she'd won a competition.

She leaned over Cloud's neck and patted him. "Oh, Cloud," she said, "weren't we a team!"

The rescue squad passed them, startling Cloud a little. "Easy, sweetboy," Faith soothed him. When she rode into the stable yard, the ambulance had already driven partway into the soggy field. The rescue team was gently easing the unconscious woman onto a stretcher. After Beth was securely placed inside, the vehicle worked its way carefully back through the gate and out the drive. It was several minutes before Faith, untacking Cloud by the stable, heard them switch on the siren.

"Nothing we can do right away, Red," said Ben Warren. "Best feed the animals."

By the time Faith and Ben Warren reached the hospital, Beth had already had a CAT scan and X-rays. A young doctor told the pair that Beth had broken her collarbone, fractured her upper arm and suffered a concussion.

"We're putting her in a clavicle strap," he said. "It's to keep her shoulders back so the collarbone can mend properly."

When Ben and Faith were allowed to visit Beth's room, she was lying with her eyes closed. There was a strap hooked under her arms which disappeared behind her back. Her left arm was in a sling. She opened her eyes and stared groggily at them in a funny, cockeyed way.

"Who painted the spill?" she asked. Neither Ben nor Faith laughed. Does she mean "Who spilled the paint?" Faith wondered.

Ben Warren just put his hand on her good shoulder and said in a quiet voice, "Beth." Then Beth smiled gently and went back to sleep. Her face was bruised but it made her look pretty, as if she were wearing rock-star makeup.

The next time she woke, she tried to get up,

saying, "Apollo didn't get grained." Ben jumped up from his chair and said, "It's all taken care of, darlin'." Then Beth sort of flicked her eyes like she'd been slapped and eased back against the pillow.

"Oh, Ben," she said softly and went right back to sleep again.

The third time she woke, she sounded like her old self. "Did anyone feed?" she asked, meaning the animals. She never worried as much about whether or not the humans had eaten.

Ben said, "Yes, we've eaten." Then he laughed and Beth laughed. Faith giggled, relieved. She said, "They're all fed, Beth." She received a grateful smile.

Then Beth turned her head to the window. She sighed. "What a jerk I am," she said.

"That's right," said Ben Warren. "You break for animals." They both laughed again.

Beth turned serious. "I'm not sure it's going to work, Ben," she said. "We get in each other's way so much."

"I'll stick around for a while, lady," said the cowboy gently. He put his big, clean hand over hers. "We'll see . . ."

12

*T*he summer horse shows were over. Beth, her arm still in a cast to protect her mending bones, began to plan for a gold cup event in Canada near Toronto. Standing in the center of the ring, she shouted instructions at her students, barely hampered by her plaster-frozen arm.

Faith and Gem would be leaving in a few days. Gem still took lessons, but her drive had gone out of it. Faith had begun to take lessons once more and she was just getting into it. Unburdened by her former fears, she was advancing quickly. Beth shook her head in surprise or looked thoughtful. She had Faith jump some low cross poles and then the two-foot coop.

Since the accident, Faith had often ridden Cloud cross-country and through the woods with other riders. She had felt easy and comfortable, as if she'd been doing it right along. But Beth no longer discussed the horses with Faith and Gem as before or included them in the planning. She was pressed for time. She ran late all day, and had begun to fall asleep in her chair at the dinner table again.

Ben Warren had finally finished the sheep's bathroom. It still smelled cleanly of new wood. Faith took her first bath in the beautiful tub. In front of the new three-way mirror she combed out her red hair, grown way below her shoulders over the summer. Maybe I'll try a ponytail, she thought. Then she felt sad. Now that she truly belonged here, it was time to leave.

Gem was in a slump. She had enjoyed the difficult riding within the confines of a ring. She had done well this summer. Now she had to leave Rambler and jumping over fences, her borrowed riding coat and blue velvet hunt cap. She had to leave Owen, her new conquest, before she had time to savor the romance.

They had returned Rackity to the woods. He was almost full grown. Beth said to just leave his door open. At first, the raccoon wouldn't leave his cage. Then, one morning, he was sitting on the back porch roof. The next day they saw him slowly enter the woods. He didn't come back.

"Good," said Beth wistfully. "He's found his real home. Maybe he'll come visit."

Now, in the evenings, Faith and her sister sat on the back porch or walked the rail fence sorrowing together. While Gem moaned about leaving Rambler and Owen, Faith thought about losing Cloud. But she also tried to imagine the strangers at home, their mom and dad, their new brothers.

The day before they were to leave, Beth brought up some of their fresh-laundered clothes, which Ben had neatly folded. She set them on top of the bed. The girls' suitcases were half packed. Beth stood watching them a moment, her head cocked to one side. Her shirt was crumpled and dusty and her dark-honey hair straggled from her scarf. She had a funny, sad little smile on her face.

"If you want to ride, go on ahead. There won't be any more lessons the rest of this week. We're busy with shearing the rams. The horses could use a workout. Take the ones that suit you. You know which tack to use. Let me know before you go."

She turned to leave but stopped at the door and looked back at them.

"I'm really going to miss you two," she said. "You've been good company—great helpers." She eyed Faith and raised her eyebrows. "I've learned some new things, too." The words didn't leave Beth easily and she began to look uncomfortable. She turned quickly and thumped down the stairs in her heavy boots.

"I'm going to miss this place, the classes—everything," said Gem. But she opted for a last date with Owen instead of a ride on Rambler.

On her way down to the stables alone, Faith said to herself, "Not a real animal person."

She thought about Beth and Ben. Beth imposed her will on things, on horses, students. Ben never forced or pushed . . . "You wind up cutting yourself." They argued all the time. Ben organized chaos to make things run smoothly. Beth moved mountains. Faith admired them both. Somewhere in between, she thought, is the road for me.

Beth had said she could have her pick of the horses for her final ride. It wasn't a difficult decision. She would take Cloud out one last time before she bid the farm good-bye.

The big black horse came to her in the field. Flattered, she pushed her face into his neck before she clipped on the lead line. "Cloud, my friend," she said.

She picked a route along the fencerow and up toward the woods. By the tree where Blackie Whiteface was buried, she stopped for a moment and said good-bye to the summer and to this place. But Cloud was eager and pawed impatiently at the earth. She pressed him into a trot.

Trees were heavily green and familiar as parents. There weren't many deerflies left to pester them as they trotted along the path.

Somewhere in the woods was an overturned boat, rotting between two trees. Faith had watched Cora and Gem jump it before. She found it with little trouble.

They paused, she and the horse. She gathered the reins, making certain Cloud saw the obstacle. He stirred beneath her. She held him, waiting, until she felt his eagerness, the excitement running up his legs and into hers.

Then she urged him forward with her calves, sitting erect until the last stride before the boat. Her hands softened forward, her legs asked. Her eyes reached out into the corridor of trunks ahead.

They soared over the boat and cantered away between the old and fragrant trees.

CAROL FENNER admired horses when she was a child growing up in Almond, New York, but she never had a chance to ride them. That didn't come until she settled in Battle Creek, Michigan, with her husband, Jiles B. Williams. She took riding lessons from a tough teacher not unlike her character Beth in *A Summer of Horses*. Now she rides her own horse, Hail Raiser, whenever her busy schedule as a writer, publicist, and teacher of writing workshops permits. Her previous books include *The Skates of Uncle Richard* and two ALA Notable Books, *Gorilla Gorilla* and *Tigers in the Cellar*.

Whoa! Here's another blue-ribbon series from Bullseye Books! Join the girls and horses of

Riding Academy ™

Jina, Andie, Lauren, and Mary Beth—the four roommates in Suite 4B at Foxhall Academy—may not see eye to eye on everything. But they do agree on one thing: they *love* horses! You'll want to read all the books in this extra-special series.

#1 • *A Horse for Mary Beth*

#2 • *Andie Out of Control*

#3 • *Jina Rides to Win*

#4 • *Lessons for Lauren*

#5 • *Mary Beth's Haunted Ride*

#6 • *Andie Shows Off*

#7 • *Jina's Pain-in-the-Neck Pony*

#8 • *The Craziest Horse Show Ever*

#9 • *Andie's Risky Business*

#10 • *Trouble at Foxhall*